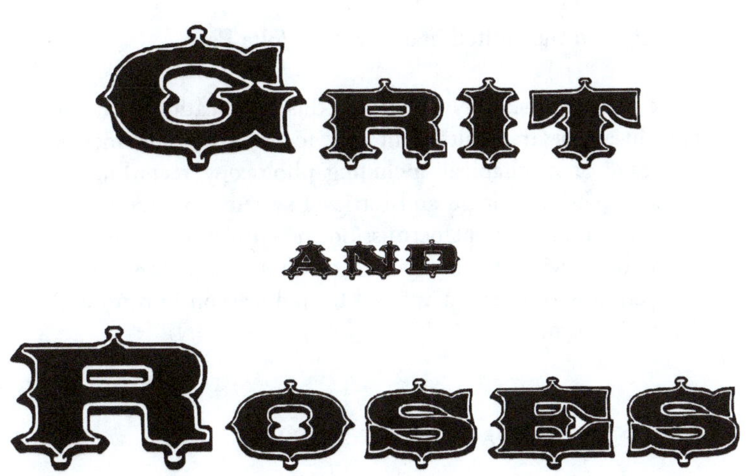

Grit and Roses

stories

by

Eugene M. Babb

Cover & Book Design: Vladimir Verano

Cover Image Credits:
Front image: © 2015 *'Empire' Graeme Maclean via Flickr.com*
Used under Creative Commons License v4.0
Back image: © 2015, *'Diner' Joe Strupek via Flickr.com*
Used under Creative Commons License v4.0

Edited by Cleta Rogers Hughes

The publisher would like to thank Janelle Retka for editorial assistance.

ISBN: 978-1-60944-101-2

Library of Congress Control Number: 2015943028

VertVolta Press
Seattle, Washington
www.vertvoltapress.com

For Cleta Hughes, Richard Dyksterhuis and Chip Hughes.
Your inspiration is unwavering.

Special thanks to Jim Ferguson and Susan Cottman
for your patience and technical wizardry.

World weary Jazzman,

His belt for a tourniquet,

Savors the needle's sting.

His sound is smoke and candlelight,

He wrings beauty out of pain.

-E.M.B.

Table of Contents

Giggin'

STEVIE WAS LATE. He really didn't give a damn about a Sunday night jazz gig in a rock club. Club owners always thought they could draw a crowd on an off night by showcasing modern jazz. There were two guys playing pool and one at the bar.

Stevie was really fat, really gifted and really stoned. Thirty five years of dedication to the music. He had studied at Julliard, but things fell apart. The constant travelling from small town to smaller town, crappy bar to crappier bar, had taken its toll. Baggy-eyed and jowly, his ten-year-old green sport coat stretched over his belly, he assembled his horn and shuffled to the bar for a beer and a shot. He needed a chemical blindfold to focus.

Opening with an upbeat samba, Stevie closed his eyes and surfed the changes, telling his story with be-bop scales and sophisticated melodies. Aggression, power and joy. The rhythm section roared like a brushfire with Stevie fanning the flames.

Broken dreams, a shattered life, declining health. Stevie had paid his dues. He was a torchbearer for a uniquely American art form.

A rim-shot on the snare drum ended the first set. Scanning the room he saw that the bartender was the only person in the place. Only three more hours to go. Weaving out the door to the parking lot, he lit up a joint and filled his lungs. Nobody sounds like me, he thought.

The last tune of the night. It was Stevie's call and he called the blues. All the misery and pain, all the joy and exhilaration of his life boiled out of his horn. Completely spent, he weaved over to the bar for one last drink.

It was two a.m. and freezing. Stevie scraped the ice off his windshield, hoped his car would start. Tomorrow was a rehearsal for a church gig.

Winter sun peeked through his bedroom window. Another booze-sick morning. There was a little cocaine left in a wrapper by the bed. He used his car key for a spoon and packed his nose. No time for a shower. He put on a tavern windbreaker, two-toned bowling shoes and jeans. Drove to Our Lady of the Lake, the sky black and white. The defroster had quit in his car and his breath fogged the windshield. He heard the organist practicing a prelude as he stumbled in. Still tasting last night's whiskey, he wandered through the church and found the kitchen. Threw up in the sink and drank some water.

The choir sounded ethereal in the resonant space of the sanctuary. Seventy-five voices sang Handel's *Messiah*. Waiting for his cue, the music penetrated him, gave him goose bumps. The coke coursed through his body and wiped away his fatigue. He dug deep and began to play. His phrases dipped and climbed, a hang glider searching for thermals. After his solo, he murmured a cadenza. Polite applause from the singers gave him affirmation. Limping slowly across the parking lot, a red hot band of pain squeezed his chest. He collapsed on the damp gravel, his pilot light blown out.

Family

It had been years since the last family vacation. On a sparkling August Monday, we boarded a ferry to Whidbey Island. Dad had rented a seaside cabin for two weeks. All of us were looking forward to sun and sand and a respite from city life.

A two bedroom house. Warped wood floors, sea breezes tickled the curtains. Rustic, comfortable. Classic northwest beach. Rocky with huge driftwood piles like giant pick-up sticks. Hypnotic rhythm of the surf and tie-dyed sunsets. The night sky was spectacular, a black dome pinpricked with starlight.

Summer fruit in the mornings, cold cut lunches with spicy potato salad. Dad would light the barbeque in the evenings and cook hamburgers, hot dogs, corn on the cob.

We had the use of a twelve foot aluminum skiff with an outboard motor. Many mornings Dad and I would putt-putt through the mist and try our luck fishing. We never caught anything, it was the conversations that I treasured.

He shared what it was like growing up in Vancouver, British Columbia: Rising at four a.m. to light the furnace, doing homework next to it because that was the warmest place in the house. Church every Sunday, falling asleep during sermons. Soccer, hockey and afternoons at his dad's store working as a soda jerk. How he met Mother. He said he was so proud of me, that my future was bright. I had never felt closer to him. Then he told me I was old enough to take the boat out by myself.

I would cruise for hours exploring hidden inlets. Hand on the tiller, salt spray sluicing over the bow, bugs in my teeth. It was intoxicating. Sometimes I would cut the motor and drift, awed by nature's panorama and humbled by its power. Killer whales like black and white submarines. Hawks gliding in spirals, rocketing down for prey. Kelp flotillas powered by the tide, the sea lions' pirouettes. And the ocean… timeless, inscrutable, the foundation for it all.

We entertained ourselves with games of cribbage and Monopoly, read paperbacks under the deck umbrella while a transistor radio played classical music in the background. Neighbors would take us waterskiing in the afternoons. Mom and Dad took long walks, sunbathed and napped. I balanced on log tightropes, dug for clams, collected starfish and went swimming every day. The time whizzed by. Mocha-skinned and relaxed, we returned to the rat race.

The calm before the storm.

Ocean of Strings

THE PHONE RANG after dinner. Ron Johnson, the principal percussionist, informed me that I had been accepted into the Seattle Youth Symphony Orchestra. The audition process had been intimidating. Afterward I had the blues, thinking I had blown it. At fourteen and a half years old, I would be the youngest member of the Ensemble.

Mom dropped me off in front of the music building on the U of W campus. I began the long trek to the subterranean rehearsal studio. The sounds of string instruments and woodwinds tuning up echoed in the stairwell. Pungent smells of bow rosin and slide oil. No one acknowledged my presence, so I climbed up to the back riser and sat down.

The conductor walked in.

Vilem Sokol was an internationally recognized Maestro, whose reputation for getting professional performances from young musicians was legendary. An imposing figure, he was over six feet tall, broad shouldered and exuded an intensity that was palpable. He was wearing a tailored white dress shirt open at the neck and pressed slacks. His Windex-blue eyes burned like gas jets.

Ron told me that I was responsible for playing multiple small parts, embellishing the music with bits of texture. The parts would be written on separate sheets of music. I would have to move from music stand to music stand to cover them. Concentration was the key. Sometimes I would have to count many bars in varying tempos before I played a cymbal crash, xylophone arpeggio or drum roll. The first piece was Ravel's *Bolero*.

I had to count eighty-six bars of music and play ten snare taps. A critical part. Mr. Sokol's arms were wind-milling and his curly mop of hair was flying as he revved up the orchestra to a blistering pace. I counted eighty-five, eighty-six… and missed it! Sokol immediately slammed the brakes on the orchestra. I waited in the deafening silence. Without looking up, he raised his baton and said "Again, from the adagio." The maelstrom of sound began again. Eighty-five, eighty-six… I missed it again! I shrank and dropped my head. "Again from the adagio," Sokol repeated. Grinding my teeth, I counted eighty-five, eighty-six… got it! Using a samurai slash of his baton, the conductor killed the music. I saw him look up at me for the first time, a cobra sizing up a mouse. Shaking his head, he remarked, "Percussionists, I could write a book."

At the break I walked to the men's room. Ravel ricocheting around my brain, I stepped up to the trough. The door banged open and in walked Vilem Sokol. He stood next to me and said hello and completed his mission. Creeping quietly to the sinks, I washed my hands. Mr. Sokol turned and faced me. An engaging smile erupted on his face. As he bent down to my level, he shook my hand and said: "I am delighted to have you in my orchestra this season." We chatted about Mozart as we walked back to rehearsal.

Downward Spiral

DAD WAS A TENURED PROFESSOR of Nuclear and Chemical Engineering at the University. Mom a gleeful housewife. We lived in a bright-white section of North Seattle. From the living room you could see the golf course and sail boats on Lake Washington.

When I was fifteen, I wandered out to the deck on a Saturday afternoon. Gardeners had just finished trimming evergreens next door and the scent of pine tar was in the air. Mom was in the kitchen, face blank. Dad was working. He had a picnic table covered with paper in front of him, a slide rule in hand. And something new: A pint can of beer. I asked for a sip. "No son, you're not old enough. Go ask Mom for a Coke." Mother's face was still blank.

During the next couple of years I noticed the fridge contained more and more Budweiser. Dad began to retire early in the evenings, was grouchy during breakfast. Then he built a wine cellar. He drank four or five large glasses of burgundy every night at dinner. Fifths of bourbon appeared in the garage. Prescription bottles lined the medicine cabinet. Early one morning I was awakened by music coming from the living room. Funereal strings floated behind a melancholy soprano. I crept downstairs and peeked around the corner. Dad was slumped on the couch, tears flowing from closed eyes. He didn't respond to my voice. I woke Mom and she called an ambulance.

Diagnosis: Acute alcoholism and barbiturate addiction, depression. Treatment was a month of inpatient rehabilitation. Mom told me that if anybody called the house looking for Dad I was to say that he was out of town lecturing. He was allowed visitors after a week.

I drove down to see him. Fall wind whistled through the car doors, leaves swirled like confetti, the sun dressed in gray. Rehab occupied two floors in a multi-tiered concrete structure near the public hospital. Inside the smells of boiled coffee, cigarettes and perspiration. Library quiet. A chunky receptionist with ochre hair and a ruby stud in her nose directed me to Dad's room. No one there. I stopped and talked with a nurse in the hall. She was young and starched and upbeat. She glanced at a clipboard, said, "He's in Arts and Crafts, number 202." Dad and a teenage vampire were making ashtrays out of black clay. Seeing me approach, the Transylvanian fluttered away. No smile from Dad, just a nod and stare. He was wearing a worn yellow bathrobe over green hospital pajamas. Threadbare slippers without socks. Trembling slightly. His skin looked sunburned, the side effect of the Thorazine they used to control his withdrawal symptoms. Conversation seemed difficult for him. I stayed for twenty minutes, wished him the best and got the hell out of there.

The day before he was released, a counselor from the center searched our house and found a pint of vodka in the upstairs toilet tank. At Dad's office she discovered a plastic bag full of Seconal. Home and workplace clean, he was discharged.

Dad refused to attend twelve-step meetings, exercise or change his diet. Shortly after he arrived home, he stormed into the dining room reeking of liquor. Mom cursed. Dad said he'd had enough of "family stress" and wanted a divorce. "Fine," she screamed, "you'll be hearing from my lawyer! Now get out!" He packed a suitcase and left. The house was sold, Mom moved into an apartment and joined a singles club. I hit the road with a cabaret act.

Christmas in Regina, Saskatchewan. Tenacious cold. Flat land, flat people. I was performing in a raggedy supper club downtown and staying at a Motel Six. One night when I was leaving for work, the desk clerk handed me a letter with an unfamiliar return address. It was from Dad. Somehow he had tracked me down. Ecstatic prose announced that he had married a "brilliant, voluptuous woman." The letter ended with, "Please come visit when you get back!" Directions and a phone number were written under his signature.

I was home for New Year's Day. Called Dad and said I'd drop by. Dressed in my only suit and brown shoes and a festive tie. Compression-started my '56 Biscayne and headed south, then east, to Mercer Island. Sparse traffic, soft blue sky. The guard at the gate grinned and waved me through. "Happy New Year Mr. Babb." Serpentine black top through luscious foliage. Million dollar homes with million dollar views of Mt. Rainier. The mansion was gaudy pink coral with pale columns. Dead chrysanthemums hung around the veranda. A curved stairway led to a mahogany door big enough to drive a car through. The doorbell rang a phrase from the *Barber of Seville* and a grim fiftyish man in tuxedo and tails ushered me inside saying, "I'm Chadwick, the houseman. Please follow me. They are waiting in the drawing room."

We walked fifty yards on dark slate flooring past dual staircases surrounded by Impressionistic paintings. Chattering Myna birds and cockatoos in silver cages. The drawing room was light and airy, furnished with heavy antique tables and chairs, a wall of bookcases, frothy green drapes. The view through the floor-to-ceiling glass was breathtaking. Dad and stepmother set down their drinks, rose and embraced me.

"This is Marion, my new bride," beamed Father. She was six feet tall, four feet wide, wore jangling emerald earrings and a long ivory gown. Bare feet with bruise-colored nails. Her face was too tight, her chest prominent. Rough blonde pixie-cut. At least ten years older than Dad. He sported a cheesy toupee flecked with dandruff. Purple sweat suit and moccasins. Both were drunk as sailors on shore leave. I drank iced tea, endured an hour of cackling grandiose conversation. Marion passed out, then Dad. Chadwick apologized and escorted me to my car. I didn't see or hear from them for twenty years.

Retired from show business, I accepted a job managing a condominium complex. On a bleak winter morning I received a call from a nurse at an assisted living facility. "Your Dad is here. I think you should come by, he doesn't have much time left." It was a nasty two story Craftsman in a neglected part of town. Smelled of urine and baked beans. In a kind voice, R.N. Shirley provided some history. "Marion owned the house. When she passed, her children evicted your Dad and sold it. He's been admitted to several psychiatric hospitals. Don't be surprised that he is still drinking. The doctors here decided that getting off booze now would cause seizures. He's down the hall in the recreation area."

He was alone. "Hi Dad, how's it going?" No recognition, no response. Bloated by booze and drugs, hammered by depression, he sat in a cracked recliner, eyes focused on a blank T.V. High-ball tumbler on the armrest. I tried again. "Anything you need Pop?"

Suddenly he looked at me. With a guttural croak he said, "Yeah. Take off so I can watch my favorite show!" He punched the remote and cranked up the volume…Bugs Bunny.

White and Black

My first day of my last year in High School. Cheap sun through stripped trees, fall's compost smell. Six buses were added to the morning queue. Integration at Nathan Hale had begun.

Blacks claimed one corner of the cafeteria, didn't mix, rebuffed any friendly overtures with profanity and threats. Fights increased, purses were stolen. Lockers were broken into. Teachers feared for their safety between classes and in the parking lot. I never went to the bathroom alone. The Black Panthers were raising hell in California, and many folks sported the berets and goatees of H. Rap Brown and Eldridge Cleaver.

Darrell was a drummer. He was seventeen. Bowling ball dark. Tall, thin, humorless. Holes in his shoes, wore the same shirt and jeans every day. We split the percussion duties in the Jazz Ensemble. He told me he hated whites. "You mutha-fucka's oppress ma people!" We didn't talk much.

His playing was liquid, hip. Complex ideas. The band grooved with him at the helm. Darrell couldn't read a note of music, but his ear was uncanny. Everything he played just sounded *right*. I invited him to share lunch many times. He always turned me down, said he couldn't maintain his "rep" if he was seen in the company of a "honky." He railed against the big band saying it was, "'nother 'zample of the white man stealin' the black man's music." Gradually, we formed a relationship based on our love for Miles Davis, the blues, and Afro-Cuban syncopation. Our ensemble won the overall competition at the Reno International Jazz Festival. He was named to the All-Star Band and was awarded a plaque. But outside of the music room he ignored me. Three-quarters of the new students dropped out that semester, Darrell included.

Three years later I was a junior at the University of Washington. Taking a break from studying, I decided to go to a snazzy nightclub that just opened. Dressed in my best suit and shoes and drove to Westlake Avenue. The club was a huge space with high ceilings. Flickering candlelight. The crowd was dense and colorful. The cocktail waitresses looked like fashion models. After buying a six dollar beer, I looked for a place to see the band. No empty seats. A back conference nook, smaller but just as grand, had speakers that pumped in the music from the main lounge. You couldn't see the musicians, but the fidelity was excellent.

The music was spare and earthy and loose. Tenor sax, acoustic bass and drums. Their use of space was amazing. I knew it took experienced, mature players to get that sound. Only a few people can pull it off.

At the end of the set, I moved into the main room, hoping to meet the musicians. To my surprise, Darrell was the drummer. He didn't recognize me at first, but then the light came on. "Hey brother-man, wha's happenin'?" He wore an immaculate gray suit, white shirt and maroon tie. Flashing brogans. "C'mon outside wit' me. I needs to getta new pair of brushes." Gulls dive-bombed for scraps, the evening was still. We leaned against his mercury-colored Town Car. He was happy, relaxed and excited. I complimented him on his performance. "Yeah man, Darius and Mulgrew hired me for this gig. It'sa dream come true. Outstandin' bread. I'm goin' to record a C.D., then off to Europe fo' a concert tour."

He talked with the manager and arranged a table for me in front. Darius, the sax man, and Mulgrew, the bassist, were full-moon white.

Bumbershoot

BUMBERSHOOT IS AN ANNUAL ARTS FESTIVAL held during late summer at the Seattle Center. Joe Fletcher, my private drum teacher, invited me down to listen to his trio play a concert at the Mural Amphitheater.

Rolling tan lawns surrounded the base of the Space Needle. The sun was kind, soft winds carried barbeque smoke and the smells of sunscreen and cooking oil. Thousands of people. College kids tossed Frisbees, families spread blankets on the grass and ate picnic lunches. Elderly couples cruised the craft booths, haggled with vendors. The stage was a square of gray risers facing the fountain, the light refracting through its mist an abstract painting suspended in the air. I helped Joe carry his drums up the side stairs and watched him set up. He was in his late sixties, Irish-white, with a military mustache and a child's smile. Embroidered tank-top, khakis, flip-flops. He looked to his left.

"Hey Don, someone I wantcha to meet."

"Yo!" said the bassist. Blonde dreadlocks framed his face, built like a rhino. He wore a black and tangerine Dashiki, jeans, worn-out Nikes. Somewhere between thirty and forty. A wine colored birth mark covered his left cheek.

"This is Geno Babb, one of my students," Joe said.

"Pleasure," Don said.

Violent brassy scales from a tenor sax startled me.

"Jorge, over here!" Joe yelled, pointing at me. "Friend of mine."

Jorge grinned around his mouthpiece, nodded and continued warming up. He looked like a teenager. Small frame and in shape, dark buzz cut. He was dressed in a solemn blue Hawaiian shirt that hung over green golf slacks, waxed loafers. He set his horn down on a stand. Fiddled with a gold chain around his wrist.

"Ready to carve some air, man?" he asked Joe.

Thumping his bass drum, Joe said, "Let's do it."

I took a seat and opened my ears.

They turned standards inside-out, building tension, releasing it into pools of beauty. Years of performing together created a unique empathy and trust. Joe and Don laid down a churning foundation, Jorge's phrases leapt and tumbled like an acrobat. Pushing and pulling and stretching the sound, they challenged each other, chuckled when someone went out on a limb. The audience hung onto every note. Knew they were hearing something special.

I picked my way through the crowd at intermission and climbed backstage. A seaplane buzzed through the plum-colored clouds, the breeze heavy and crisp. Joe and Don were splitting a pitcher of beer and having a hushed conversation. Jorge smoked and studied a sexy blonde swiveling toward the pizza counter. Joe waved at me.

"I just talked with the guys. You're gonna play the last set," he said.

"What?"

"You'll learn more from playing with them than I could teach you in a year."

My pulse doubled.

"I'm gonna get some more beer." Joe jumped off the stage and headed toward the concession area. Don looked up.

"No sweat kid." he said. "You'll be fine. Ignore the crowd. Punch out some strong time and LISTEN. Do you savvy?"

"Ab…absolutely."

Adrenalin pumping, I followed them out front and sat down on the set. Adjusted a mounted tom and cymbal stand. Don picked up a mike, tapped on it to see if it was working and made an announcement.

"Ladies and Gentleman! We have a special guest sitting in for the last few tunes. Give a warm welcome to Geno Babb on drums!"

Whistles and claps, a baby cried. I was sweating blood.

"Green Dolphin Street, four-four Latin." said Jorge. He chose a medium-up tempo.

The drumsticks felt like dumbbells, my feet were concrete blocks. I rushed and dragged, missed all the breaks. Panic locked my brain. Consummate professionals, Don and Jorge bulled through the arrangement. By the time I got some traction we were at the coda. I played two bars past the ending.

Stepping back behind the drums, Jorge whispered in my ear. "Lay out for the next one, get yourself together."

Red-faced, I studied my knees. They played a ballad, "When Sunny Gets Blue." Sweet and poignant and powerful. Standing ovation.

Don glanced at me. "Okay man. "Blue Bossa" You start and we'll jump in."

Four measures and my right stick caught on the snare drum rim and pin-wheeled skyward. Feedback screeched from the monitors. I saw tendrils of smoke curling from the sound system. Scruffy stagehands came running with extinguishers and soaked the cables. Amazing grace.

I apologized for my performance.

"Not necessary," said Jorge. "We've all been there."

"Don't be too hard on yourself," Joe said. "My first time out was a disaster. Now you know what it takes to play on this level. You learned the hard way what your weaknesses are and that's positive."

I said nothing.

Each of them reminisced about their beginnings, shared a laugh, packed up their instruments and left. Clowns juggled balloons, howls of excitement from the rollercoaster. I walked slowly to the parking lot, hands in my pockets. Twilight's arms wrapped around my shoulders. Who in the hell said this too shall pass?

Cornish

After thirteen years of playing the drums, I decided to pursue a career as a jazz musician. But improvisation was a new frontier. Some guidance was needed. One of the most innovative percussionists in the country was teaching at Cornish Institute of The Arts in my home town. Jerry Granelli agreed to see me for one session.

Arriving early, I wandered around the school looking for Jerry's classroom. Cafeteria aromas, stunning a cappella voices. From above, the thunderous stampede of a ballet class. No drums. Confused and anxious, I approached the nearest door. Someone was playing a piano in the room. Dark melodies with machine-gun technique. When the music stopped, I cautiously knocked. Jerry Granelli opened the door.

Without saying a word he ushered me into his studio. He was a lanky man with violet eyes and a cop mustache. The space was crammed with a baby grand piano and two sets of drums, the shelves on the walls overflowing with aluminum tubes, Chinese prayer bells, ancient cymbals and gongs. Wood blocks, cowbells and triangles littered the window sill. Jerry said, "Let's play."

He stopped me before I could sit down at a set of drums. "No, no. We are going to improvise a duet using the instruments around you. Use as many as you want. Play an introduction and I will follow." I grabbed a small triangle and beater. My introduction consisted of a few pings and a roll. He had a Latin gourd with a wooden stick and played a pattern of scrapes and clicks. We pinged and scraped together for a while, then he walked over to a gong and struck a mighty blow. I stopped playing immediately. "No, don't stop. I am making a transition to the next movement." He picked up one of the aluminum tubes and sawed it with a violin bow, creating a ghostly wail. I had no idea what to do. He said, "Think of the music as a balloon we are trying to keep in the air. It can move in any direction, but do not let it hit the floor." We continued for a few more minutes, Jerry producing a myriad of sounds from three more instruments and me flailing on a timbale. "That's enough," he said. "Please sit at the drum set and we'll try something less abstract."

Relieved to be playing a familiar instrument, I sat down and picked up a pair of sticks. He rummaged through a folder, withdrew a page and set it on the music stand in front of me. "Play that for me," he said. It was a picture of a tree. Shutting my eyes, I started playing. It was a Herculean effort with pitiful results. Jerry's face was granite when he nodded. "Okay. One last exercise and our time will be up."

He sat down at the piano and said, "You and I are going to imagine ourselves in the Taj Mahal. We will play what we see."

Long silence. Jerry looked at me and asked, "What's wrong?"

"I'm trying to figure out how to get there," I replied.

A wisp of a smile passed over his face. "You're already there man, you're already there, you see?" Jerry played the Taj Mahal, I clanged and banged. As I was leaving he said, "Remember. If you don't hear anything, don't play anything."

Driving home, I understood the gravity of his last remark. Mr. Granelli was being very subtle. What he really meant was if you don't hear anything, you don't have the music in you.

Film and Lenses

Ink barely dry on my Bachelors Degree, I looked for a job. Figured the best opportunities would be found through an employment agency. So I contracted with an outfit called Business Careers Associates.

I interviewed with shoe stores, a lumber yard, appliance outlets. File clerk positions at insurance companies, lot boy at car dealerships. Struck out. Bills were piling up. I called Uncle to see if he was hiring for his chain of camera shops. A self-made millionaire, he started selling cameras at grandfather's pharmacy on Kitsilano Beach, B.C. Soon there were twenty-five stores across Canada, and he was expanding in the U.S. He agreed to a meeting at his condo overlooking Lake Union.

The driveway was a mile of denture-white pavement that meandered to a mountain of smoked glass and steel. I was driving an old Ford. Rear window missing, carpet scraps covering flayed upholstery. The valet growled, "Park around back!" Toxic stare from the concierge. He called the penthouse to confirm my appointment and followed me to the elevator. My ears popped during the ascent. Gilded doors opened, revealing Norm Babb.

Six foot tall with a pear body. European cut suit. Thin hair, fat smile. "So you want to be in the photography business."

After ushering me into a living room the size of a tennis court, he strolled to a mahogany bar. "Wanna drink?" It was 10 a.m.

"Beer would be good," I replied.

He mixed a screwdriver for himself and gave me a Danish brew in a frosted mug. Every wall was covered with pictures he had taken. He was a master of light and color. Heart-stopping sunsets from all over the world. Waterfalls you could hear. Orchid close-ups that looked like paintings. The largest photo captured a stunning brunette languishing on a beach. Aunt Beverly. Nude.

Norm said he was looking for someone to manage his operation in the States. Would that appeal to me? "Absolutely!" I lied. Delighted, he told me I would train at his store in Northgate Mall.

My shift was 11 a.m. to 9:30 p.m. six days a week. Will Smithe was the manager. He had been a combat photographer in Vietnam. Early thirties, affable, pudgy. Cigarette hoarse and a Beatle haircut. Low man does the scut work: I cleaned display cases, cameras and lenses, the bathroom.

Slide film, print film, movie film. High speed black and white, slow speed color. American, Japanese, German. Eight, sixteen, thirty five millimeter. Polaroid. Shutter speeds, apertures, wide angles and zooms. I took copious notes, feigned interest. I started working the counter.

I used a low-voltage approach. No pressure. Customers ate it up. Within six weeks, I was number two in sales. Twelve weeks, assistant manager. Will was ecstatic. I was despondent. Photography never fascinated me, I just needed work. Faking passion was wearing me down.

I went to the Musicians Union and put my name on the board. Hooked up with a show band doing a "Tribute to Elvis." Norm never spoke to me again.

Prestidigitation

Dad took me to see a magic show at the Masonic Temple.

It was warm and musty inside. Light fell from ceiling spots, illuminating a wall of red velvet that draped an elevated stage. After a recorded trumpet fanfare, the curtain rose, revealing a short table covered with white cloth. The music changed to strings and a tornado of greenish fog appeared from the wings. The magician strutted out from the vortex.

He was a giant. Easily seven feet tall. Long slicked-back gray hair. Boxer's nose twisted over a psychotic smile. He wore a beautifully cut fuchsia tuxedo and high topped black tennis shoes.

Thousands of playing cards flew through the air. Gaudy silk handkerchiefs waltzed around him, changed into flapping doves. An endless cascade of silver dollars flowed from his hands. Multicolored balls floated in space and vanished. Out of an empty hat jumped a rabbit. For the finale the table levitated and disappeared. Astonished and excited, I knew that was what I wanted to do with my life.

The library was a tremendous resource. I checked out every book on magic. Studied its history from court jesters to

Houdini and Blackstone. Bought cards and learned slight-of-hand. Went to the magician's supply store in town and used money I earned from mowing lawns to purchase tricks. And practiced, practiced, practiced. I put together a short routine and performed for family and friends. The next step was joining the Pacific Coast Magician's Association.

Harvey Long, a retired vaudeville illusionist, was the president of the local chapter. I called him and he invited me to his home for an audition.

The house was at the end of a shaded brick lane, disguised by thick woods. Turrets and stained glass and cedar siding. Brass gargoyle knocker on an iron-strapped door. One tap and it opened. Harvey invited me in with a flourish. He was small, wide and happy. Close-set teal eyes. Maybe in his late seventies. He was dressed in a pale sweat suit and worn sandals. He led me up a dim staircase to a large den. Harvey tipped a book out from a case and a panel slid open. Inside was a miniature elevator.

We descended to a scaled down version of a club built in his basement. Small stage with pleated curtains, a dozen cocktail tables with chairs, banks of lights. I set up and ran through my show.

"You have a good start, but there are too many rough edges. If you're interested, you can attend meetings and the other members will help you polish your moves."

Twice a month the association met at Harvey's place, exchanged ideas, tried out new tricks, and critiqued stage presentation. The other members were older and more experienced, but they were all supportive and seemed to enjoy helping me improve. My confidence soared. Finally after weeks of rehearsing, Harvey said I was ready for a public performance. He booked a weekday matinee gig for me at University Hospital.

I tossed and turned the night before the job. Unusual, I never had insomnia. I dressed in a white suit, white shirt, and white shoes. Red bow tie for flash. I packed my gear in a duffel bag and tucked cab fare into my wallet. My mouth was parched. More than just butterflies. My act had been tightened and tuned by professionals, I had it down cold. What the hell was going on? I waited for my ride at the curb. Thunder clouds muffled the sun, lightning ripped the horizon. The cab was late. The driver was a mellow black kid. He rolled a cigar stub around chapped lips. When I told him my destination he laughed, said, "Good idea man, ya'll look like ya need a doctor."

Cross-town traffic was glistening sludge. I arrived at the hospital with just a few minutes to spare, was directed to the auditorium by a smug candy striper with too many teeth. Sweat dripped off the end of my nose. The show must go on. I jogged down a shiny hallway, shoes chirping on the waxed linoleum. Pushed through double doors.

A huge open room. Cute animal posters on the walls. The storm battered the windows, its flashing light created a strobe effect that gave me vertigo. Thirty or so people waited. Patients in robes and gowns, a few on gurneys with I.V. drips. Quiet as a water glass. Gulping air, I started the routine.

My opener was producing a plaster-of-paris skull from a scarf. The skull was tucked under my left arm. As I turned the scarf to show the audience that it was empty, the skull dropped from under my coat and fell to the floor. Some giggles from the crowd, mostly silence. My brain froze and my knees knocked. Deer in the headlights. I tried to remember the next trick, fumbled out a deck of cards and promptly spilled them. I threw my stuff in the bag and marched stiffly out of the room. Fortunately there was a taxi waiting at the entrance. I dodged Mom at home, said everything went fine. I called Harvey and resigned from the association. The symptoms abated overnight. It was the first volley of my long battle with anxiety, the shadow that walked with me through the rest of my life.

Palm Desert

I LEFT SEATTLE under an orange sky with fifty dollars in my wallet. A lounge act in Palm Desert needed a sideman. My first out-of-town gig since graduating from High School. Twenty-four hours after I left home, I crested the San Bernadino mountains and drove down into the desert.

Heat shimmered off the ivory sand. Date palms and sagebrush and jackrabbits. The air blowing through the van's windows smelled like hot tar and baked fruit. I found the motel the group had booked for me. It was a dilapidated 1950's motor court. The doors were different colors, their brass numbers askew, patches of tarp flapped on the roof. Three vagrants shared a bottle of wine in front of the office. The desk clerk was a cranky octogenarian in a wheelchair. Skinny and toothless, beak for a nose. She wore a long-sleeved brown t-shirt with glitter sprinkled on it. Her cap had "I Love Vegas" on the brim, her legs covered with a beach towel. I signed in.

"Number thirteen, Sonny. Don't plug the dam' crapper!" she said when she tossed me the key.

The room wasn't too bad. Clean but worn. Water dripped from the air-conditioner and the shower head. Soft mattress.

Fresh sheets and pillow cases, courtesy coffee packets. Odd smell of gasoline and peanut butter. I took a nap, showered and shaved. Dressed in pressed beige slacks and a red shirt and my new shoes. Walked down the street to check out the club. Warm winds caressed my face, tousled my hair.

A blonde-stone drive split a lush stand of banana trees. The club looked like a mansion from the Deep South. Wrap-around veranda with hanging baskets of ferns and orchids. Dark shutters, marble columns white as frost. Limousines were parked out front, the drivers talking and smoking. Inside was blue and cream and cool. A vise clamped down on my shoulder.

"Where da ya think you're goi'n pal?" I slowly turned my head, saw an olive-skinned King Kong stuffed into a tuxedo.

"I'm the drummer in the band, thought I'd come early and check the place out."

"That's fine," he said, "but ya gotta wear a coat an' tie to be in heah. Are ya hungry?" "Starving." I said. He walked me into the kitchen and introduced me to a tough looking little guy in a chef's outfit.

"This is Frankie," he said. "Tell'm what ya want, then sit over dere, he'll bring your food. Employees get free dinner ev'ry night. My name's Mario Rossi. I own this joint. If youse need anything, anything at all, just come to me, unnerstand?" I thanked him and ordered a five course meal.

The room was always jammed. The band's repertoire was as thick as a phone book, they could field any request. Always a thousand dollars in the tip jar. When Mario found out where I was staying, he moved me into a poolside bungalow at a ho-tel he owned in town.

I jogged in the mornings, sunbathed in the afternoons. Performed for adoring crowds and made scads of money. On the last night of the gig, a drunk staggered up to a cocktail waitress and started fondling her. He was at least three hundred pounds, really aggressive. Without thinking, I jumped out of my chair, got between them and threw a forearm into his throat. And got knocked on my ass.

Mario said, "I got it man!" and rammed him through the back door. I went out to the alley behind the kitchen to catch my breath. Saw the drunk propped up against a garbage can. He looked like he'd been hit by a train. His head was a bloody balloon, his clothes were rags, his arms and legs at unnatural angles. Two bodybuilders in leisure suits threw him into the trunk of a Chrysler. When I went back inside Mario ordered me a Jack Daniels, patted my cheek. It was the first time I had seen him smile. "Ya must be part Sicilian. That waitress is my niece."

The other band members were going to pick up their regular drummer in Omaha. Mario helped me load the van. I thanked him profusely for his hospitality. He nodded once. Another cheek pat. I disappeared into the desert light.

A few days after I got back a local booking agency contacted me and requested an interview. I dressed in a new suit and drove to Bellevue. The agency was in a tower of mirrored glass. The slinky receptionist took my arm and walked with me to an office in the back. She tapped on a thick oak door.

"Who's there?" a rusty baritone asked.

"It's your two o'clock, sir."

"Send'm in."

There was a small, tight man with rhinestone eyes sitting behind the desk. Auburn razor-cut hair. No smile lines. His knuckles were scar tissue. Gorgeous butter-cream topcoat.

"Siddown kid," he said. I sat. "I'm Ralphie. I work for Mr. Rossi. He says you're a stand-up guy." He slid a typewritten page towards me. "Here'sa two month contract wit' the jazz quartet at da Hilton. You wanna sign it or what?"

The day I signed was my eighteenth birthday.

Country

When I was attending college, performing six nights a week was out of the question. However, weekend gigs were available. A guitar player from a previous group referred me to a band leader who wanted a drummer every Friday and Saturday night from August through New Year's Eve. White shirt, dark slacks and dark shoes were the uniform, kick-ass country was the music.

The bar appeared through the mist like a U.F.O., flashing neon and noise. It had no name. There must have been twenty motorcycles lined up out front. Light rain beaded on the chrome and leather, iron horses sweating and steaming at the end of the trail. Two signs were posted by the entrance: "Topless Beauties" and "Please check your weapons at the door."

Nostril-searing funk. The dancers were doing a narcotic slink to a rock and roll tape blasting from speakers the size of refrigerators. Stiletto heels, g-strings, freak show chests. One had all her teeth. Their smiles didn't reach their eyes. They sashayed off the stage and the rest of the band arrived.

Three guys, all over forty. Jocks gone to fat. Frayed cowboy hats over basset hound faces. Belt buckles the size of dinner plates. They plugged in their guitars and tuned up. The pedal steel player looked at me and said, "Hope ya can play, kid."

Tight harmonies, toe tapping guitar riffs. No dead air between songs. I made it through the first set with no mistakes.

I was eighteen. The drinking age was twenty one. Because of the liquor laws, I was supposed to spend my breaks on the stage or outside the club. As I headed out to my car, the band's leader waved me over to a back table. His face was expressionless, his voice a cement mixer. "Where in the hell did a young punk like you learn to play country so damn good?" Then he cackled and punched my arm. "You're a natural, kid. Only one problem. You look like you don't eat enough." He turned to the bar and whistled, like he was hailing a cab. A spectral man materialized. Very thin, very nervous. His hair was a greasy mop and his mustache covered his mouth. Stuck to his denim vest was a name tag that said, "Buzzard." "Get my drummer a burger basket and a tall beer, put it on my tab," bellowed my boss. He winked and said, "You stay inside on the breaks and sit in the kitchen. The dancers don't want ya on the stage and I don't want ya out in the parking lot by yourself. My name's Terry. Welcome aboard."

The patrons were a mosaic of hardcore bikers, suit-clad professionals, laborers, and down-and-outers. I felt like I was performing the soundtrack for a Fellini film. Surprisingly, there was never any violence. Everyone just wanted to have a good time. The staff treated me like family. Buzzard always greeted me with a beer. The dancers fussed over me, asked how college was going and baked me brownies. Most of them were single mothers. Terry told me to stay in school and study hard. After work the bouncers walked me to my car. What initially looked like a gig from hell turned into one of the most enjoyable experiences of my life, personally and musically.

And I have never, ever, tasted better cheeseburgers.

Screwed

A RATTY CLUB in the foothills of the Cascades. Choking smoke, sticky tables, loggers, cowboys, beer and wine. The crowd booed every tune that wasn't rock or country. This was our last night of a week-long gig. I saw a tall, muscular Asian man in a black three piece suit order coffee at the bar. He sat in front of us, clapped and smiled during the set.

I walked into a storage room to get a fresh pair of sticks out of my trap case. This loudmouth who'd been hassling me followed. Shaved head, stained gray strap overalls, no shirt. Motorcycle boots and a teardrop tattoo. He spun me around and grabbed me by the throat.

"You assholes didn't play my song!" he yelled.

He started shaking me, slammed me into the wall. Suddenly, his eyes bugged and he dropped to the floor. The Asian guy was behind him, brushing a piece of lint off his lapel. "Pressure points on the neck. Effective, yes?" he said. "My name is Anthony Wong, may I buy you a drink?"

"I've been traveling all over the state looking for a group to perform in my nightclub. You would be a perfect fit," Anthony said. "I'll double your last salary. First, a two week trial engagement. If I make money, a long term contract. Interested?"

I said, "Deal." After the last set, Anthony gave us directions to the club and three hundred dollars for traveling expenses. He bowed slightly, slid into a pristine maroon Cadillac and motored toward the freeway.

The club was located on the Washington coast. I chose the scenic route. Evergreens danced in the breeze, the Pacific was rolling gray velvet. My VW Bus wheezed and rattled, the water's tangy scent seeping through its vents, sky the color of huckleberries. Consulting Anthony's map, I exited the highway and began climbing a brand new asphalt road to the top of a bluff. No houses, no stores, infinite wilderness. The road dead-ended at a beautifully carved cedar block reading, "Anthony's," with an arrow pointing to a narrow brick driveway that flowed through the forest. Miles later, the building appeared.

It was a replica of a Native American long house. Course-grained wood siding, peaked cedar-shake roof on a rambling one story structure surrounded by sculpted rhododendrons. Just as I shut off the motor, six bulky men dressed in tight T-shirts and yellow slacks surrounded the van. The oldest one approached me, said "You band?" I nodded and stepped out. "We carry equipment to stage, park your car," he said. "Mr. Anthony say you have dinner, then set up. He see you later." I tossed him the keys and we walked inside.

An exotic young woman wearing a turquoise dress with red orchids embroidered on the sleeves ushered us to a table with an expansive view. The dining area had high-beamed ceilings, glass walls. Dark blue carpet contrasted with light wood paneling. You could see fishing boats and water skiers and people walking on the beach. Anthony walked out through the swinging kitchen doors and joined us. "You are welcome to eat in the dining room any time," he said. "Accommodations are on the house. You play Tuesday through Saturday, three one hour sets a night at nine, eleven and one. Any questions?"

"What kind of music do you want?" I asked.

"Play the songs you enjoy. If you are happy, my patrons will be too," he replied. "Ms. Kwan is my assistant. Contact her if you need to speak with me." He nodded at the hostess and returned to the kitchen.

The lounge was spacious, pink evening light fell through skylights. Citrus and ginger in the air. Linen tablecloths topped with flickering red candles, walnut chairs with cushions the same shade of blue as the dining room rug. The bartender made small talk with a young couple waiting for their dinner reservation. Our instruments were placed neatly on the roomy stage. State-of-the-art sound system and spotlights.

Each of us had a suite with a king-sized bed and whirlpool tub. Through my window I watched an eagle feeding its chicks in a towering spruce, the sun melting into the ocean.

No slow nights. An army of bartenders and cocktail servers barely kept up. Anthony worked the crowd, bantering and pouring champagne. Two weeks felt like one. We signed a three month contract. Anthony said, "You take a week off with pay, go home and rest. See you next Tuesday."

We drove back to Anthony's in a thunderstorm. Lightning sutured the clouds, thunder like cannon volleys. The two hour drive took three. When we arrived there was no welcoming committee. In the lounge another group's gear was on the stage. I marched into Anthony's office. He was sitting at his desk, gazing at the rain tumbling down his window.

"What's going on?" I asked.

"Simple," he said. "I found a group I liked better than yours and they will work for practically nothing." "We have a signed contract with you!" I exclaimed. Shrugging, he said "So sue me. Now get the hell out of here."

Our Union representative said there was nothing she could do. Anthony had declared bankruptcy.

The Reservation

One of the most memorable gigs I ever played was on the Puyallup Indian Reservation at Bob's Country Nightclub. The band before us had been fired mid-week and we agreed to finish the engagement.

The lounge was located forty miles southeast of Seattle. It was a huge cinder block barn sitting in the middle of a hay-field. No windows, no beer signs. The door looked like it had been used for target practice. Rows and rows of folding tables, a few crusty red vinyl booths. Pomade and stale beer stench, bowling-alley acoustics. The stage had two green spotlights and one yellow. The green spots were broken. For security, a quartet of wrestler types armed with pistols. The jukebox wailed old time rock and roll. While loading in, I was told by a waitress that Bob Running Bear was the tribal chief, his son Danny managed the bar. She picked up a phone, said a few words. "Danny'll be right down."

Danny was mid-forties, thin and sharp. He wore a brand new Levi jacket and blue jeans, snakeskin boots. Long midnight-black hair in pig tails. Turquoise earrings. "Hi, I'm the boss. You guys smoke marijuana?"

"No sir," I answered.

"Excellent. I *hate* potheads." He returned with two pitchers of beer and some glasses and set them on a table. "The band gets free beer as long as you don't abuse the privilege." We nodded agreement and finished setting up.

Opening night. The place was almost full. Virtually all the patrons were Caucasian. Worn folks dressed in pressed work shirts and slacks, athletic shoes or boots. Clean and quiet. It's important to set the tone of the evening from the very first tune. I chose an original composition entitled, *Sadie*. In-your-face rump-rocking blues. Nobody danced. Danny ran up and crooked a finger at me to join him in his office.

Acrid pipe smoke choked the air. "Burnin' riffs man, but I got a few requests."

"Go ahead," I said.

"You know that Dorothy thing? Uhhh… Somehow over the rainbow?"

I nodded yes.

"Right on. Now… how 'bout that chick on the beach song, the girl from whatsis?"

"Ipanema" I replied.

"Yeah, that's it. What do you call that stuff?"

"Bossa Nova," I said.

"Yeah, that's what I want. Classy."

I dug out some old fake books and redid all the set lists. Tossed in some Tom Jones and Ellington and Basie. The dance floor stayed full until closing time.

One night I walked outside to eat a sandwich and stretch my legs. Silver light, humid. Bullfrog conversations. From out of the shadows, a figure walked right up to me. Really short with a perfect ponytail. Dressed in worn Army fatigues. Bland expression. He said, "I'm Reuben, what's yer name?" I introduced myself and told him I was in the band. "Far out. Gotta smoke?" I gave him a Camel and lighter. We talked about cars, women, getting old.

"Come inside and I'll buy you a beer," I said.

"Naw, I'm workin'." He flipped the butt into a ditch. "My job is ta make th' rounds outside the club. Bob gets bomb threats."

The last night of the job, I noticed a new couple among the regulars. He was way past middle age, homely and fat. Penny-colored skin. He wore an outfit like a cattle rancher. She was a gorgeous model-slim blonde decked out in scarlet short-shorts and a bursting orange bikini top. A mauve baseball cap shaded searing blue eyes. Maybe nineteen. She banged down Tequila and chain smoked. They danced to every tune. They were at the bar when I ordered a drink. The guy turned and said, "Hey pardner, I'm Bob Running Bear and this here's my wife Maisie. Super good music! You're making me a pile o' money!"

I thanked him for the compliment and finished my drink. He excused himself and walked over to a security guard stationed by a side entrance. Maisie batted her lashes, burped, leaned over and unzipped my pants.

End of the Road

Twelve thirty a.m. No refrigerator in the room, so I'd filled the sink with ice from the machine. Bologna, cheese, and my last quart of Budweiser floated in the slush.

The club was a short distance from the motel. I walked by the closed tourist traps and fish and chip stands. Surf whispered under a melancholy moon. Cats yowled, light brine breeze. Sand worked its way through the holes in my loafers. I pushed through the warped door, removed my cloth jacket and sat at the bar. The stool wobbled, its cushion was slit. Smells of cheap whiskey and chili. As usual, no customers. Tony the barkeep raised his eyebrows and I nodded. He set a pint that was half foam in front of me. He was a wimpy guy, probably late fifties. Short face, flat ears, crescent of scraggly grey hair. He wore a tank top and pajama bottoms. A Mickey Mouse tattoo waved from his left forearm. "Last night of the gig, right?" he asked. I said nothing, went up to the stage and sat behind my drums.

Tito the bass player and Ollie the guitarist got up from a table and joined me. Both were barely twenty-one and on spring break from school. I hired them off the "At Liberty" board at the union. Tito was an animated Caucasian with a diamond in his right incisor. He read Schopenhauer on the breaks. Frail and Asian, Ollie chewed gum constantly. Thick lenses in his glasses magnified his eyes. The whole week they played with heated intensity.

We kicked off the set with *Salt Peanuts*, a ferocious hard bop tribute to Bird and Diz. I blocked out the grim atmosphere and embraced the sound. Next tune was a ballad, *Naima* by Coltrane. The music laughed and cried as we sketched a portrait of a beautiful woman. I saw Tommy gesture from the bar.

"Just play one more fellas, then ya'll can head for home." We closed with the blues. Dirty, gut wrenching, cathartic. Tony paid us. Just enough to cover gas and some groceries. He said, "Wish it coulda been more, but I didn`t make no money with you guys." Tito and Ollie packed their gear and said good-bye. They were leaving that night, had to be at college the next morning. I was too drunk to drive, so I didn't break down my kit. I planned to head out the next day.

I wound my way back to the motel. Mustard light from the street lamps, a freighter chugged in the distance. Sharp wind slashed through my clothes. I let myself in, turned on the lights, and looked in the bathroom mirror. Skin like a corpse. Hair falling out in patches. Red-rimmed eyes and rotting teeth. I was twenty eight. Eleven years in the music business and I was still playing the same low-level clubs. In my heart, I knew it was over. Sitting on the bed, my head bowed, I said a short prayer ... and buried my dream.

Holiday

Three thousand miles from home. December 24th. Cold, no snow. The last notes of "Jingle Bell Rock" rang in my ears as I stepped off the stage. I ordered eggnog spiked with rum and wondered how I was going to fill the next day. The other musicians in the group were spending Christmas with their girlfriends. I bumped into Mo when I picked up my parka from the coat-check girl.

She was a regular on Tuesday nights. Swarthy, petite, maybe forty, conservative dresser. Laugh like a semi-truck grinding gears. Never drunk, never sober. Always arrived by herself, even though she wore a wedding band. I asked her about that once. "My husband and I have a deal. This is my time to do what I enjoy." Mo really loved to dance. All styles. She was graceful and energetic and felt the music, would stay until closing. When she found out I would be alone for the holiday, she invited me to spend it with her family.

Mo picked me up at noon in an old brown Cadillac, its paint abused by the New Jersey winters. A few minutes on the Turnpike, then into a working class neighborhood. Identical bungalows stood shoulder to shoulder, all decked out in lights and decorations. Pick-up trucks, vans, children's toys in the driveways. She parked in front of an immaculate yellow and green house and we crunched across the lawn to the door. Her husband and two children welcomed us with hugs and cups of hot cider.

Inside the air was scented with roasting meat, lemon furniture polish and cinnamon. The tree stood in a corner, lights winking. Her husband was a postal worker. He looked like a middle-weight boxer. Blonde hair cut short, bright eyes, workout suit. The kids were slim and dark, had infectious smiles. Both wore new sweatshirts and jeans. One girl, one boy. Sixteen and eighteen. They wanted to know what it was like to be a member of a travelling band. Cider flowed, and I shared stories about all the characters I had met, the cross-country trip from the last gig in California, the pompous bandleader and living out of a suitcase. The meal was turkey and ham, twice-baked potatoes, green bean casserole. Mo was one hell of a cook. It had been close to five months since I had eaten home cooked food. To top it all off, we had pumpkin pie and coffee, sat around the tree and listened to Mo's husband play the piano. Jazz inflected carols with incandescent improvisations. Afternoon blended into evening. They all wished me well and told me to stay in touch. Mo drove me back to the YMCA, the urban glow a beacon in front of us.

"OUT OF SERVICE" sign posted on the elevator door. Six flights to the room. It was chilly, quiet. I lit a candle and looked out the window at the stark cityscape below. Frozen rain began tapping on the glass. A homeless man pushed his shopping cart along the sidewalk, screeching scripture.

Oroville

IF YOU WANT TO WORK full time as a musician, booking agencies are a necessary evil. 'Solid Gold Talent' procured us a gig in Eastern Washington, a few miles south of the Canadian border. We jammed four musicians, a sound system, instruments, and luggage into a twenty year old van and drove six hours. Compared to the mountains, trees and lakes of the West, the East was fallow and desolate.

Hundred degrees in the shade. The tavern was a concrete building with a flat roof. Chunks of it were missing. The parking lot was a sand box strewn with beer cans and cigarette butts and glassine envelopes. Duct-tape repairs on the windows. The door was screened and bent, propped open with an empty keg. Inside, distorted Country Western music from a battered boom box on the floor. Low ceiling and warped tables with full ashtrays. The aromas of fried meat and dirty clothes and manure. The bartender had "Fuck You" tattooed on his knuckles and wore a leather vest rotted at the armpits, his face a mug shot. Sun-scorched white trash and migrant workers guzzled tap beer and Loganberry wine mixed with Coca-Cola. Couple of the guys ogled the vocalist. After a sound check, we drove to our accommodations. Apple and apricot orchards bordered the road, their trees heavy with fruit, the air a blast furnace. The band house was a listing bungalow with necrotic siding. Lizards napped in the dirt driveway. No air conditioning. The television had a coat hanger for an antennae and broken screen. Rancid bathroom and aggressive mosquitoes. The fridge was lukewarm. We went to a thrift store for sheets and towels. Bought a gallon of bleach and scrubbed everything twice and tried to get some rest. Dirt bikes raced up and down the street.

We showed up on time for the first set. Our singer was dressed in a short, black cocktail dress. The rest of us wore suits with white shirts and gray ties. On her way to the stage, some yahoo asked Susan, "How much for a blow job, honey?" Smiling sweetly, she picked up his drink and threw it in his face. We opened with Ellington, followed by Streisand and a Beatles medley. Barrages of catcalls mingled with shouts of "rock and roll!!" In twenty minutes the bar was empty. The manager called us into his office. He was on the back side of fifty, obese, smoldering.

"What the hell is going on? I ordered a hard rock band and you play a bunch of gay shit? This ain't no damn cruise ship. Ya'll are losing me money! Yer fired!" Unable to get a fresh group on such short notice, he told us to finish the rest of the week and get out.

The waitresses made no money and blasted us with hostility. Tires were slashed on the van. We slept too much, hardly ate. The last night of the engagement we showed up in jeans and tank tops, played one set and high-tailed it out of there. We kept the agency's commission and used it for gas and food on the trip home.

Our first stop was 'Solid Gold Talent.'

The sign on the boarded up building read "Coming soon: Wong's Mandarin Cuisine."

Bouncer

La Grande, Oregon, is a sleepy little burg a few miles north of Pendleton. Dung-brown hills, dead trees, rattlesnakes and a truck stop. There was only one place you could dance to live music, a grimy twenty table lounge on the outskirts of town. We were booked there for two weeks. Ray Jones was the bouncer.

The customers were all white. Ray was the color of roof tar. He was soft spoken, well built, with a trimmed goatee and a flashing gold incisor. A hair over six feet tall, maybe twenty-five years old. His work uniform was a white shirt under a red vest, black jeans and black cowboy boots. His left hand was missing the little finger. Thunder clouds lurked behind his eyes.

Late July is the height of fire season in eastern Oregon. One sweltering Friday, volcanic plumes of smoke and ash erupted in the hills surrounding the town. When I arrived at work, the parking lot was jammed with filthy pickup trucks and campers, license plates from Montana, Idaho and Washington state. The bar was teeming with smokejumpers called in to battle the fires, rough looking wiry guys reeking of wood smoke and testosterone. They were drinking hard and fast, getting rowdy. One of them got in Ray's face and called him a nigger. Ray politely asked him to be more respectful or he would be cut off. The jumper poked him in the chest, told him to go fuck himself. In one fluid motion, Ray grabbed the guy's wrist, twisted it until the bones snapped, and threw him out the door. The other smokejumpers immediately calmed down.

I finished packing my drums on the last night of the gig and offered to buy Ray a beer. Curiosity got the better of me and I asked him how he had ended up in this two horse town. Looking at nothing, he told me his story.

To escape the poverty and violence in Biloxi, Mississippi, he joined the Marines, taught hand to hand combat stateside, and was shipped off to Vietnam. He said it was the most beautiful place he had ever seen. Twenty shades of green, rainbows of tropical flowers oozing hypnotic perfumes, exotic birds singing you to sleep. That was base camp. Two weeks later his platoon jumped in a truck and headed into combat.

In a dead voice, Ray described G.I.'s with Viet Cong ears hanging from their belts, exploding children, the constant drug use. While on night patrol, the point man snagged a trip wire for a booby trap. Ray said everyone in front of him was shredded by the mine. Shrapnel tore off his little finger. He was alone in enemy territory.

The medic's kit was intact, so he bound his wound and pumped himself full of morphine, hoping someone knew where he was. All night he listened to VC marching through the jungle around him. Vipers slithered through the bushes he hid in. Insects used him for a buffet. He prayed and ate speed to stay awake. At daybreak, he heard the whip-whip-whip of a helicopter. It hovered directly above him, its searchlight blazing. A distorted voice with an American accent boomed from the copter's loudspeaker, saying they were there to pick up survivors. Ray said he had been warned that some North

Vietnamese could speak perfect English. Stoned, terrified of being captured, he shot out the light. A burst of bullets from the chopper demolished the ground cover around him. Another voice with a Southern drawl materialized.

"Knock it off hard ass, y'all wanna to git outta here or what?" He was awarded a Purple Heart and sent back to the States. When he arrived in New York a group of war protestors spit on him. He bought a jalopy and drove west. The car broke down in La Grande, so he decided to stay, said it was easier being black in Oregon than Mississippi.

The toughest guy I ever met sauntered out into the midnight haze.

Chanteuse

It was a Wednesday. Ladies' Night. Usually there were only a few people for a few hours, quiet conversations, then the place would empty at eleven-thirty. Not this Wednesday. It was a zoo.

The seating capacity was eighty. There were over a hundred crammed inside. Ladies liked Margaritas and Daiquiris, so the blenders behind the bar thrashed non-stop. Every tune we played was accompanied by their dissonance. The air was dense with smoke and saturated with cologne. The alcohol triggered personality changes.

Demure classy women became foul-mouthed and belligerent. Shoving matches and violent threats from the guys. They used pocket change for tips, complained to the bartender about weak drinks. The police were summoned twice. Fortunately, the room cleared by midnight. She arrived in time for the last set.

Pale as a mannequin. Probably thirty. Luscious and distant. Brunette with million dollar legs. She wore an oriental black sheath. Vermilion dragons were stitched parallel with the slit. She sat in the booth closest to the stage, smoked pastel cigarettes in a silver holder. Drank martinis straight up with olives. There were scars on her wrists, like pink zippers. She listened with her eyes closed, swayed with the rhythms. She requested a ballad, "Someone To Watch Over Me." We played it for her. She bought us a plate of snacks and rounds of drinks.

"Thank-you so much!" she said. "That song means a lot to me." The pain in her smile tore my heart.

For the next couple of months, she came in every Wednesday at the same time, requested the same tune and left immediately afterward. She never gave her name. Then on Christmas Eve, she asked if she could sing her favorite tune with us. There were no customers, so I said okay, hoping she wasn't a drunk who thought she was a vocalist. The pianist played the opening arpeggio.

Her voice had terrifying beauty. Perfect pitch. An operatic range. Dynamics from whisper to growl. We were stunned. I offered her a job that night. She accepted and said her name was Lila Brown.

Word got around about the lovely torch singer. Standing room only six nights a week. All the traveling jazz acts would come in and study every nuance. A representative from Pablo Records showed up and wanted to record her live. He flew in an engineer from L.A. and taped a month's worth of performances. The album went gold and Lila was nominated for "Best New Artist" in *Down Beat* magazine. We went on a five city tour of the West Coast, received rave reviews, returned home to a house gig in a luxury hotel. But things started to unravel.

Sometimes Lila was a few minutes late for work. Her smile was smaller, her hair and make-up sloppy. She drank more and only wanted to sing a few numbers. Little things made her blow up. One evening, she went to the Ladies Room and didn't come out. I sent a waitress to check on her. She came out running and grabbed the phone, her shoes tinted crimson. The medics said Lila was barely alive. An ambulance took her to the psych ward at Harborview. She was allowed visitors a month later.

I drove down to see her. The sky was gray and white, rain poured through the evening. The hospital was a huge rust-colored complex overlooking Elliot Bay. I parked in the garage and took the elevator to the eighth floor. The doors opened onto a hallway that only had one door. It looked like steel and was painted lime green. A small plastic window imbedded with a wire grate was in the center. The cold eye of a video camera looked me over. A red button in the jamb had a sign over it that read, "Ring for Entry." I pushed it and heard a tinny voice from a speaker in the ceiling.

"What do you want?" I said I was there to visit Lila Brown. The lock buzzed and I entered. It was absolutely silent. Slight smell of pine mixed with tomato soup.

In front of me was a glassed-in nurse's station. Behind it was a long breezeway with a dozen doors on each side. The doors were all closed. No patients walked around. The booth was manned by two orderlies. They were big, black, friendly. Max and John on their name tags. I was told to empty my pockets and remove my belt. The flowers and candy I brought were confiscated. Along with my pocket knife. Max said, "Let`s go see the songbird."

Our shoes squeaked on the shiny yellow linoleum. Lila was in the last room on the left. Max unlocked the door and said, "I'll be right outside if you need me. Stay as long as you want."

She was sitting on a cot in a space the size of my bathroom. Both forearms were in hard beige casts. She was wearing a grungy pink terry robe with no sash over a hospital gown, paper slippers and a plastic shower cap. Ferocious body odor. A paper plate with toast crusts and a Styrofoam cup with a tea bag floating in it were on the floor. Her eyes looked strange, no pupils. Medication, I thought. She didn't recognize me. No response to, "How are you, Lila?" I held her hand and sat with her. She never moved or spoke, just stared through the bars on the window. I left after twenty minutes.

Sleep never came that night. I noticed dawn seeping through the blinds. And realized that for Lila, sunrise always meant darkness.

Barkeep

All by myself on a Sunday night in Jersey. Drowning in boredom and loneliness. I decided to ride the rails to New York City.

With a mechanical hiss, the train disgorged in Grand Central Station. Autumn wind slapped me as I stepped into the street. The air was ripe, the street a river of cars and people. Predatory feel. I couldn't find any live music, so I ducked into a shoebox-sized lounge to escape the chill.

No patrons, Jerry Vale on the jukebox. A small bell, like you see on hotel desks, sat next to the cash register. I tapped it and waited. Through a bead curtain at the end of the bar shuffled a tiny man. Seventy-ish, urban wizened, nasty cough. The drinking age was eighteen, I looked fourteen.

After checking my identification, he wheezed, "Whaddya want?"

"A shot and a draft please," I answered.

He poured my drinks and a double shot for himself. When the music ended he turned on a battered T.V. screwed into the wall. Yankees against the Tigers. We drank, munched peanuts, traded comments about the teams. Just a couple of guys enjoying a game. No other customers came in. Four boilermakers later, the Yankees won. It was late, I was wasted. I paid my tab and started to leave. The little guy stopped me and asked where I was going. I told him. He shook his head. Said it wasn't safe to walk by myself to Grand Central. He called a cab and gave me money for the fare. He said, "Anytime you're in the city drop by. The drinks are on me."

Early morning at the train station. Intermittent brake squeals, hydraulic sighs. Scent of buttered popcorn and pretzels. Only a couple of travelers and a maintenance guy swinging a mop. I looked at the schedule. Two hours until my ride home. I passed out on a bench. Something smacked the soles of my shoes. Hard! Through my whiskey fog, I saw one of New York's Finest. Young. Gigantic. Italian features, his billy club spinning. "Youse can't sleep here kid. Got any I.D.?" His eyes defrosted when he saw I was an out-of-towner. He bought me coffee and a roll, told me if I needed to use the restroom he would accompany me. "Nevah know who might be in dere." He checked on me during his rounds and walked me to the boarding platform. Trash blew around our feet, the tunnel's warm breath comforting. He found me a seat and gave me a salute. Cop-walked back to the waiting area.

Looking out the back window of the train car, I watched New York's grin fade slowly to black.

Rich Folk

When you put together a new group, the first gigs are always out of town, performing in worn-out bars for burned-out people. Subsistence pay. This is an opportunity to tighten up the music, experiment with arrangements and build a résumé. After four months on the road, our agent called with a step up. The Seattle Tennis Club. Wealthy folks had connections to lucrative corporate parties, wedding receptions, political meet and greets. On a luminous August afternoon, we loaded up and rumbled toward the lake.

A manicured neighborhood without sidewalks. No people, no parked cars. Eerie silence. The houses were hidden behind tall hedges. Driveways were guarded by ornate gates and red-eyed security cameras. The entrance to the club sat at the end of a cul-de-sac. White gates and a guard shack bigger than my apartment. The guard slid open the window and said, "Who the hell are you?" He was old and anorexic. Face like a water moccasin. Blue uniform and a tie with pistols embroidered on it.

I said, "We're the musicians performing for the cocktail party."

"Well la-de-da," he said. "Have any drugs or weapons?"

"No sir."

"Swell," he replied.

"Follow the lane to the left and park that piece of crap behind the kitchen. Trevor will meet you." He picked up his phone, raised the barrier.

Immaculate blacktop guided us to a low powder blue building. Fragrance of freshly mowed grass and charred meat. Platoons of staff running around like ants. They were all Hispanic. And angry. Fifteen minutes passed. Thirty. Finally a smooth-looking Aryan kid in tennis whites appeared. "I'm Trevor. You're playing on Court One. Hurry up and move your equipment." It was a city block to the court. The sun was ferocious. By the time everything was set up, we were hot and thirsty. We changed into formal clothes in the van, flagged down a scowling waiter and asked for a pitcher of ice water. His right foot tapped.

"Are you members?" he whined.

"No, we're the band."

"Bye bye!" He spun on his heel and sashayed toward the tennis courts. Five minutes before the first set. I grabbed an empty wine carafe and glasses off a table. Walked over to a hose bib and filled the carafe with water.

The band sounded good. In tune and swinging, dramatic dynamics. Lots of two-steps, waltzes and show tunes. Tony Bennett, Dean Martin. There were at least five hundred patrons, all fat and slick and drunk. Gleaming jewelry and raucous laughter. In the middle of the second set, while we were playing, a matron wearing a sweat-stained maroon pantsuit sidled up to me. Flimsy gray wig, chemical tan, flammable breath. She yelled in my ear: "Pway some Elvish!!!" Trying to concentrate on the tune I said that management didn't want any rock and roll, just easy listening. She bellowed, "Ash-hole!!" and toppled over a fern. Our final set was interminable. Immediately following the last note we began hauling the instruments back to the van.

Dinner was included in the contract. Faint and dehydrated we went into the dining room. I approached the maitre d and told him about the meal arrangement. Glacial glare, tight tuxedo. "Not my responsibility, talk to Trevor." It took half an hour to track him down. He was teaching a scrumptious older woman how to serve, flexing and flirting. I mentioned the food and asked for the paycheck. Trevor threw down his racket, mumbled, "Yeah, yeah, yeah. Follow me." He hustled us into an office lined with animal heads and pipe racks, flopped open a notebook and scratched out a check. Then he directed us toward a groundskeeper's hut. "Your dinner's in there, in the fridge. Have a nice day."

Buried in a jungle of paint cans, rakes, fertilizer bags, sprinklers and netting, a rusty refrigerator clung to life. Inside were a bottle of olives, a dented can of balls and half a dozen small packages wrapped in plastic. Labels on the packages said, "Ham and Swiss" and "Egg Salad." Sandwiches twenty days past their freshness date. We pooled our change and dined at the candy machine in the lobby. Climbed into our ride and burned rubber to the gate. All of us gave the security guard a one finger salute.

The check bounced.

Cross-Country

Five weeks in Palm Desert, California. My first road trip as a professional musician. Dry balmy heat, exceptional accommodations, performing for wealthy people who appreciated Joe Williams, Broadway show tunes and Stan Getz. I had a short stay back in Seattle and switched bands. I flew to L.A. to hook up with them. The next gig was in New Brunswick, New Jersey.

We rented a U-Haul and left California at three thirty in the morning, heading east across the Southwest. Crossing the border into New Mexico, we were treated to a beautiful sunrise. Pink, mauve and gold dripped on the landscape. The snow-capped Rocky Mountains beckoned in the distance. Reptile farms, Native American art shops and mom-and-pop diners led the way. Filling up at a gas station in the Texas panhandle, I felt the chill of prejudice.

It was 1972, and we all had hair down to our shoulders. Two guys meandered out to our truck. "Y'all ain't from round here are ya?" said a behemoth with a hunting knife on his belt. His partner looked like a muscle-bound Gila monster.

"No sir," I replied. "We're headed to the East Coast to work." Tumbleweed ambled by, sand in the wind.

"Ya'll ain't hippies are ya?"

With a smile on my face I said, "No sir, we`re musicians." Gila spit a stream of tobacco juice a few inches from my shoes.

Our guitarist asked, "You like Willie Nelson?"

"Damn right we do!" answered the giant. While Ed played *Whiskey River* I frantically filled the tank.

Fat boy exclaimed, "Goddammit, ya sound jes like 'im! Ya'll have a safe trip ya hear?" Muscle-bound grinned and farted.

The Great Plains were behind us and we entered the Pennsylvania Turnpike. Lush trees lined the highway, the sun a dappled laser. Tired and wired, we crossed the New Jersey state line about one in the morning on a Monday.

Only a few streetlights were lit. Ground glass dusted the street. Packs of dogs foraged for food in the gutters. Abandoned buildings glowered at us as we headed for the club. A few wrong turns later and the Travel Lodge sign appeared through the gloom.

The bar at the hotel had a postage-stamp stage, only enough room for the drums and organ. Once we were set up, we realized that there was barely room to stand. If you moved more than a few inches, you would bump into a piece of equipment or another band member.

Room and board were not provided. Each of us had to find a place to stay. I rented a room at the Y.M.C.A. for twenty bucks a week. Ruptured mattress and a community bathroom with leaking fixtures. Grim ghetto view out the window. The heat was rationed, shut off between midnight and four a.m.

The hotel manager really liked us. But the grind wore us down. The married band members started cheating on their wives. Booze and drugs became food. We began sniping at each other, arguing over the stupidest things. Performing lost its appeal, homesickness weighed heavily on all of us. At the end of the final week, we decided to break up and drove four days straight back to Los Angeles. I caught a red-eye flight back to Seattle.

Unable to find a straight job, I joined another touring band.

My next job was in Winnipeg, Manitoba.

Bad Trip

When I was seven, my elementary school class attended a rehearsal of the Seattle Symphony Orchestra. The bus pulled up in front of the Opera House and we were directed into plush seats and told to be very quiet. Mesmerized by the powerful sound from the stage, I listened with rapt attention to the percussionists. The timbre of the xylophone, the delicate shadings of the snare drum, tympani creating the roar of an approaching train with a propeller-blur of mallets. My tumultuous affair with music had begun.

With my parents loving support, I started taking private lessons and joined the school concert band. The challenges of rehearsal and performing live concerts gave me a rush I had never experienced. I got hooked on the sound. Hooked on applause too. Then I heard Buddy Rich play with his big band. The next day my folks bought me a used set of drums and I joined the stage band in my junior high school. I was free to improvise my own part in the compositions and didn't have to share the spotlight with other drummers. My first paying gig was in a community theatre production of *Gypsy* when I was thirteen years old. Some musicians at school formed a garage band to play at mixers and To-Los and asked me to join. It wasn't jazz, but I learned rock and roll and the blues. I was as popular as the quarterback on the football team.

The high school I attended had an award winning jazz ensemble. In my sophomore year I passed the audition and competed in all the West Coast jazz festivals. We took first prize in every one, and at the Reno festival I was honored with the drummer's chair in the All-Star band.

While working a part time job at a library, a friend called and said there was an opportunity to join a real touring group. The draft lottery for the Vietnam War had claimed the drummer and the leader needed someone right away. I tried out and was hired on the spot. One month after graduating from high school I was a full time working musician, heading out on the road to work in nightclubs and bars across the country.

Six nights a week, five sets a night, your day off spent travelling to the next refuge for lost souls. The factory work of a club player. I smoked marijuana all day and got drunk every night. Five months later I quit and returned home suffering from gingivitis and malnutrition. I healed up and decided to pursue a career in jazz.

I studied with a local drummer and honed the rudiments. I went back to playing popular music in bars to finance demo tapes. Sent those tapes to dozens of record companies. Nada. I performed at every venue for improvised music within a thousand miles. No steady gigs, no record deal.

I gave up, quit playing and admitted defeat. Not only had I failed to achieve my goal, I had wasted years of my life. The demo tapes were tossed in the garbage. The drums were packed up and banished to a back closet. I didn't answer the phone, listen to music or watch television. I lived off minimum wage jobs. All I wanted to do was sleep. An integral part of my identity had died. The steps of the grief process were steep and tortuous. Inch by inch, I crawled to the summit of acceptance.

Sometimes I look back …

But I don't stare.

Disillusion

Freddie Cruz finally came to town. My favorite jazz trumpeter. His picture hung over my dresser. I had all his recordings, never seen him in person. Been saving money for months from my job shelving books at the library.

He was performing at an old-time bar near the docks. The moon was low and veiled with pale gray clouds. Boats bounced in the harbor, the air rank with diesel fuel and the smell of crabmeat. Fake I.D. and a smile got me in. A small crowd of listeners and a bartender inside a room the size of a hatbox. Red and black décor. You could hear the ferry's fog horns through the walls. My beer was warm and served in a soapy-tasting schooner.

The back-up musicians filed in half an hour late. No Freddy. They began with a tired blues riff, had robotic stares. Stains on their ties and stubble on their faces. Each of them played a long, lackluster solo. People shifted in their seats and looked at their watches. A guy with a trumpet case walked through the door and sat down in a booth. He wolfed down three shots, signaled for more.

I didn't recognize him.

Gone were the urbane good looks and the New York couture. Skin like Blue Cheese, scary-thin body in a garbage bag suit. Burn holes on the lapels, unbuttoned cuffs. His shoes needed shining, his hair was chrome-colored cotton-candy. The band started playing another mundane number. Freddie snapped his fingers to the rhythm. Blew out his spit valve and played.

Coal instead of diamonds. His trademark mellifluous phrasing reduced to anemic shrieks by a booze-swollen embouchure. Customers left, shaking their heads, their drinks unfinished on the tables. The band quit playing after two tunes and went outside. Hoping Freddy would improve, I stuck around for the next set. Watched the cocktail servers wipe down the tables and snuff out candles. The bartender sucked on a toothpick and cleaned his nails.

Freddie and the group returned after a thirty-minute break. From across the room I could smell weed in their clothes. I could hear Freddie whining about the club, his salary, the motor home he had to travel in. He complained about the "shitty crowd," said he was throwing "pearls before swine." I was the only one in the audience.

The music was sloppy, uninspired and weak. Adding insult to injury, Freddie murdered *My Funny Valentine*, his signature tune. After the final piece, the sidemen left and Freddie went to the bar. Wanting an autograph, I approached. I bought him a whiskey and asked him to sign an album. He growled an obscenity and ordered the doorman to throw me out.

Lying in bed, I listened to his Grammy-winning discs until dawn. Freddie Cruz's trumpet, an angel's voice, his notes floating like crystal ashes in the air. I heard his lust for life, his humor. Felt his power.

Drudge

ANOTHER BAND DISINTEGRATED. Unemployed again. I had to find a job immediately or lose my apartment. I saw an ad in the neighborhood paper, looking for housekeepers at a small motel. Forty bucks a week less than playing music, but it was steady work and close to home. I applied and got the job.

It was a three story building one block off the main drag in the University District. Sixties ash-gray stucco, burnt out bulbs in the sign, hamburger joint across the street, a crumbling bodega next door. Twenty apartments for rent by the day or month. Inside, water damaged lime walls, aquamarine carpet begging for help. The smells of fabric softener, full diapers and corn bread. Mac and Ellie Johnson were the managers.

Mac was a Native Alaskan, favored snap-button Western shirts and cracked cowboy boots. He was fast-food heavy with a girly mouth. His wife was a petite Alabama saltine with dentures the color of puddle mud. She dressed exactly like Mac … everyday.

The shift was eight a.m. to five p.m. Monday through Friday. Two hours then a break, two hours then lunch, two hours another break, two hours until quitting time. I dragged my butt out of bed at six in the morning and walked a mile to work. An average day was cleaning ten apartments, each having multiple beds, a kitchen and bathroom. Laundry was done on site in a huge, clanking commercial washer. The dryer blew fuses constantly. Mountains of sheets and towels. Wash, dry, fold, then into the storage closets on each floor. Up and down three flights of stairs. The hallways were sweltering in summer, frigid in winter.

It was Bedlam. Deadbeats, stoned college kids, hookers way past their expiration dates. A suicide. Police sweeps looking for illegal gambling parties and cars broken into in the garage. There were holes punched in walls, angry husbands looking for unfaithful wives.

On a good day tips totaled fifty cents. I stole bathroom tissue, soap, cigarettes and change from the cash register. Sometimes food and liquor were left in the rooms. Many shifts I gratefully ate and drank the leftovers. And considered jumping off the roof. Twenty-six years old and a college graduate, scrubbing toilets and doing laundry. The depression and guilt were bone-crunching.

Early on a damp fall morning, Ellie told me to take fresh towels to Room 305. I knocked and a raspy male voice said to enter. The guy was a few years older than me. He had a diamond stud in his left ear, wiry brown hair with a full beard, a red plaid shirt tucked into thrift store jeans. A hip lumberjack. I noticed a guitar case leaning against a chair. His head bobbed to music coming through tiny earphones. Taking a shot in the dark, I told him if he ever needed a good drummer to look me up. The earphones came off. He introduced himself as Gary Melcher and said he needed a drummer right away. Lunch hour, I sprinted home and brought back a demo tape from my last group. Gary listened to the tape. Grinning, he said I passed the audition. He showed me a signed contract for a permanent gig at a ritzy hotel. Cocktail jazz five nights a week. I jumped on the offer. Goodbye, toilets!

The lounge was elegant. Dark mahogany paneling contrasted with lighter colored wood tables. Cushy wrap around booths. Candles in crystal holders infused the room with an intimate ambiance. A glass panel took up the whole west side of the space, revealing a panoramic view of the harbor. No cigarette smog, no television over the bar. Coltrane's horn whispered from invisible speakers. The stage was roomy, the PA system precise. Classy-sexy waitresses served drinks with thousand-watt smiles. An absolutely perfect place for performing.

We were fired after the second week. Evidently the corporation that owned the hotel thought they could increase their profits by changing to country and western music. If we wanted to pursue a breach of contract suit we had to contact their lawyer in Manhattan. Knowing we didn't have the resources to fight a mammoth conglomerate, the band dissolved. Gary went home to California. I swallowed my pride and made a phone call.

Hello, toilets.

Angel

OCTOBER OF 1972. I was working on the Eastern Seaboard and staying downtown at the YMCA. Mabel's Pantry was a tiny restaurant nearby. Greasy tables, greasy food, bitter coffee. Depressed waitresses slammed plates down in front of you, smoked while they worked. Without a car, this was it for breakfast, lunch and dinner.

On my first day off, stir-crazy in the small room, I decided to check out the neighborhood. Looking out my window I saw rain bouncing off the street, autumn leaves like confetti in the air. I put on my rubber boots and pea coat and frayed Mariner's cap. First stop: Mabel's. The sign on the door said "CLOSED SUNDAYS." Block after block, I looked for a grocery store or 7-Eleven. Lightning flashed, thunder rolled. Raggedy cats and fat rats peered out from creepy alleys. A newspaper delivery truck sped by and soaked me from head to toe. After two hours of searching for food, I struck out. Shivering and sniffling, I resigned myself to eating the crackers I'd stolen from the diner the day before. Suddenly the aroma of grilled meat and onions floated in the air.

My nose led me down a dead-end side street to a small group of street people lined up outside the doorway of an abandoned building. I waited in line, stomach growling, mouth watering. When I got to the doorway, a black man was cooking hot dogs on a grimy Hibachi. Junky thin, elephant ears, left eye stitched shut. He wore a stained Stetson with holes in the brim and a long camouflage duster. The brace on his right leg sounded like musical spoons when he moved. "One or two, man?" he asked.

"Two please," I answered.

"Onions, mustard?"

"Yes, please."

He looked up. "A polit 'un. You not f'om 'round heah are ya?"

"New to the area, sir," I replied. He nodded and handed me two gorgeous dogs on slices of French bread piled high with chopped onions and dripping brown mustard.

"Thank you sir, what do I owe you?"

"Pay what ya can. If y'all are short, catch me nex' time. I'm heah evra Sunday aftanoon 'til dark." I dug in my wallet and gave him two fives.

"Thas way too much fo' two dogs. Come back and yo' nex' meal is free."

"Yessir."

"An' don' call me 'sir.' Name's Walter." He grinned and offered his gloved hand.

The next Sunday I was first in line. Fall was in full swing. Low cold sun, crisp breeze. A city truck ambled along, its crew vacuuming out street drains.

"Here ya go, man. Two dogs all th' way, on da house." Walter said, his eyes blinking in the smoke. He looked behind me, saw almost a dozen people waiting.

"Whoa. Really a crowd taday. If'n I buy ya a drink later, wouldya lend me a hand servin' these folks?"

"Glad to help, Walter," I said. He cooked, I put the brats in bread with condiments, handed them out to the tragic parade. Ancient winos, their hands shaking so badly they could hardly hold the food. Vacant-eyed bag ladies. Twelve-year-old hookers in hot pants and over-the-knee boots, faces coated with outrageous make-up. Amputees struggling on homemade crutches or rolling on boards with casters. Daylight died and the street lamps popped on, bathing the block in a mean blue light. "Thas it fo' taday, come inside fo' that taste," Walter said. He poured water from a plastic jug on the coals, ushered me through the door. I heard something scurry across the floor. Cobwebs hung from the ceiling like clouds of thread. Fierce latrine smell. He produced two folding metal chairs, pulled a pint of Mad Dog 20/20 out of a coat pocket, unscrewed the cap and offered it to me. The wine was wonderful. Tart and sweet at the same time, the alcohol a warm blanket.

"Why do you do this, Walter?" I asked. He scratched the stitches on his eye, straightened the braced leg.

"I been dam' lucky in my life, decided ta pay it fo'ward, thas all. What are you doin' here?"

"Playing in a road band, trying to make it as a musician," I replied.

"A travelin' man, huh? Here, let me give ya somethin'." He reached under his shirt and came out with a St. Christopher medal on a cheap chain. "This'll protect' you on ya'lls journeys." I put it around my neck and thanked him. "No sweat Junior. Comin' back nex' Sunday?" I nodded. "See ya then, pardner." I walked back to my room. A bottle rolled down the street, clinking on the pavement, the air thick with the smell of approaching rain.

Every day off, I spent the afternoon serving hot dogs. Winter tiptoed in. Slippery crust on the walkways, vicious winds snapped the flags on the buildings. Downtown was gray, brown, white. Walter invited people to eat inside the building. His easy attitude calmed down even the most disturbed individuals. Sometimes he passed around a thermos of coffee. At the end of the day, we had the traditional drink, talked jazz. Walter was in love with Dinah Washington. And Miles' second quintet. "That Tony Williams be a cyclone, brother. Listen to that cat an' LEARN!"

On my last day I went to say good bye. Snow fell steady and light, dampened sound. It squeaked under my boots, dusted my glasses. When I reached Walter's building, the front door was nailed shut. "Condemned" spray-painted in red on the wood. No Walter. I waited a while, shuffled to stay warm. Two teen prostitutes wheeled around the corner.

"Have you seen Walter?" I said.

"Naw man, haven't seen 'im inna week. Wanna date?" the short one said. I declined. Giggling, they sauntered away.

Heavy snow now. I navigated back through the swirling flakes, the St. Christopher medal an ice chip on my chest.

Director

Barely surviving with a minimum-wage job, I needed some extra income. The gods smiled. A keyboardist I worked with occasionally called in a panic. He needed a drummer immediately for a pit band gig in a musical. I had just enough time to make rehearsal.

The People's Theater was in an ancient neighborhood just south of Pioneer Square. Massive revitalization was underway: construction cranes scraped the sky, growling cement trucks, jack-hammer percussion. Vacant lots piled with rubble, palatial condos perched on glass peaks. Traffic was thick and listless, the sun a villain. I had to use a parking garage, ten bucks for three hours. Loaded my gear on a dolly, dodged cursing workers and rolled through the hot breeze into the lobby.

Gauze-white walls and a cathedral ceiling made the small room feel big. Colorful playbills chronicled previous productions. Bowls of flowers on side tables sweetened the air. Next to the ticket booth, double-doors of polished steel etched with "Theater Seating." The doors opened outwards and a young woman strutted out, lit a small cigar. Short and thin, peach Mohawk over a rat face. She wore a navy blue mini with tattered stockings, scuffed patrol boots. Her low cut tank top revealed a tarantula tattoo on her left breast. No light in her eyes.

"Hi, would you tell me where the musicians are?" I asked.

She ignored me, scratched the spider, stared through a cloud of nicotine.

I said, "Are they backstage?"

"DO NOT FUCKIN' TALK DIRECTLY TO ME!!" she roared. She stomped the cigar into the linoleum and slithered out a fire exit. I pushed my drums into the theater.

Plum-colored curtains with silver borders spilled down over a six-foot-tall stage. Close to three hundred folding seats upholstered with black fabric, sound absorbing carpet, meager glow from ornate wall sconces. Lighting technicians scrambled up webs of scaffolding and experimented with gels. I could smell hot plastic and sawdust. The piano player emerged stage left. Late forties, lumpy, stained gray sweatpants, torn down vest. He climbed down and pumped my hand.

"Glad you could make it, man." He said.

"Glad to be here, Doug. Where do I set up?"

He nodded stage right.

Three office partitions were placed on the floor in a "U" shape, the open end facing the stage. The closed end was filled with a synthesizer. I was concerned about space for my kit.

"No worries, you'll only need a bass drum, hi-hat, snare and ride cymbal. It's just the two of us. We'll work on the score the next few days, the actors and director will be here next week for a run-through" he said.

Knuckles and Love was the title of the show. The music was an odd combination of country, heavy metal and sugary ballads.

"What's the plot?" I asked.

Doug sighed, rubbed his face.

"Aliens take over this small town. The locals send them packing. Back story is a romance between the Sheriff and a Holstein."

"Jesus, who wrote it?"

He whipped out a program.

"Written, directed and music composed by Mazal Klein. Says she's from New York City. There's a picture," he chortled.

"Let me guess. Mean looking chick with a Mohawk?" I said.

"Yup, how'd you know?"

"We've met."

First day of full rehearsal. Up in the balcony sat a distinguished looking man in a sharp suit. He leaned forward intently. Doug and I nailed the overture. The opening scene went smoothly, non-sequiturs for dialogue. Ms. Klein paced and smoked and muttered. She had a bullhorn hanging from a strap around her neck. In the middle of scene two, she used it.

"Stop right goddam now!"

Tension filled the silence.

"Hey you, drummer boy. You're playing too many fuckin' reds and blues. My music DEMANDS orange and green. Got it?"

My ears burned, Doug rolled his eyes.

"Okay," I said. "I'll try something else."

"Good. Again from the edge."

I switched from ride cymbal to hi-hat.

Bar twenty-nine she ran over within a few feet of me, raised the bullhorn.

"No, no, no, no, NO! Orange and GREEN! Christ, all ya gotta do is fuckin' FEEL IT! I don't have TIME for this crap. Let's keep movin'."

More incoherent lines, haystacks sprouting space men, square dancing on a Chinese flag. Klein picked her nose and shimmied with the rhythms. She yelled, "cut," and applauded. "Beautiful shit, people. Everyone take twenty." Her head swiveled toward me. "Except YOU, Ringo." The guy in the balcony left.

Doug lifted his chin.

"Want me to stick around?"

"No thanks, I can handle her," I said.

He reached into a cooler, poured Coke into a glass of ice and gave it to me. Walked into the wings.

Mazal Klein got in my face. Her breath was onions and garlic.

"You're fuckin' up my tunes man! The colors are fuckin' WRONG! You don't know what the FUCK you're doin'!"

I looked her in the eye, sipped the Coke.

"Nothing to SAY, dick head?" she screamed.

I stood up slowly, poured the drink down her shirt and walked out. Summer rain bled from a canopy of thin clouds. Driving away, I listened to an Errol Garner CD, my anger dissipating.

There was a message on my machine when I got home. Doug was laughing so hard he could barely speak.

"That dude in the balcony? He was the president of the theater board. He reamed Klein in front of the cast and fired her. We're gonna do *The King and I*, Interested?"

Locals

We were in a small town on the Alaska coast. The only gig we could find on short notice. Fourteen nights straight. That was bad enough, but then the bar manager said, "Remember, jam sessions on Saturday afternoons. Two until four."

On the first Saturday my clock radio woke me at one p.m. with a sax blowing blue ice. It was the middle of the night for a musician. I stumbled across the mildewed carpet to the bathroom and banged my funny bone on the door frame. I showered and brushed my teeth. Dressed in a wrinkled white shirt, faded black slacks and running shoes. Rammed down a triple screwdriver.

The sky was a purple and pink parfait. Salt in the wind, boats tapping against the docks. I could feel the hot pavement through my shoes. Seabirds wheeled and argued. The bar was a tired weathered box with doors scarred by kick marks. Inside, air conditioners coughed a warm breeze tainted by burnt pizza, whiskey and cheap perfume. The rest of the band was already there, looking tired and put-out. Same for the bartender and waitress. The doorman had a sign-up sheet for people that wanted to perform. We played the first set, watched some patrons file in. A few scribbled on the bouncer's list and looked expectantly at the stage.

First up was a woman. Short and fat and young. She was wearing a loose green-gold dress that looked like drapes from a gothic mansion. Sandals, no hose, chipped bloody toe nails. "Sheila" was scrolled on her neck. From a ripped manila envelope she pulled out sheet music, passed it to the piano player. The tune was *Strange Fruit* by Billie Holiday. "I do this'n E flat minor," she growled. "Change to C-sharp at tha' bridge, 'kay?" She conducted the intro like Bernstein, the microphone in a choke hold. Her voice was cats mating. Stopping in the middle of the first verse, she started over. Boos and hisses from the crowd. A beer bottle sailed past her head and shattered on the wall behind us. She scooped up her music, screamed, "you guys suck!" and waddled out the back exit. We played a rock and roll medley, hoping to keep what was left of the crowd.

Next was a drummer. Coveralls, no shirt, logging boots. Completely hairless, dangerously fat. Smelled like bait. Really jumpy with bulging red eyes that blinked incessantly. He said, "I'm deeeep inta tha blues man. Gotta lotta LOTTA shit in my life! Let's ROCK!!" He counted off a slow tempo, raced to a galloping one. Loud and out of control. Impossible to play with, so the guys just sat back and turned it into a drum solo. It took thirty seconds for him to run out of ideas. He continued for six minutes. Broke two pairs of sticks and split the bass drum head. All the tables were empty. After patching the head I glanced at my watch. Enough time for one more.

The guy carried a dented guitar case in his right hand. His left hand was missing. From the case he removed a cowbell covered with grime. He was gray-bearded with a platinum pony tail under a watch cap. Boat shoes, bourbon face. "I work alone fellas, just gimme a chair." I gave him my drum stool. He perched delicately, took a swallow from a flask he produced from his coat pocket and hummed into the bell. Sounded like a cross between Gregorian chant and a chainsaw. When he finished he bowed to imaginary applause, snickered. Switching gears, he sang the chorus to Roger Miller's *King of the Road* accompanied by spastic choreography. Flask again. For a finale, he barfed on his lap. Only eight more days on the ship of fools.

Sugar

It all started with chocolate pie in the summer of 1957. I was three years old. After a light supper of salad and cold chicken, Mom served dessert. A two inch layer of almost-black filling, topped with whipped cream, sprinkled with chocolate chips and piled on a flaky crust. I had never tasted anything like it. Mom cut me a sliver. The first mouthful of the chilled pudding, the crunchy-chewy chocolate chips and cream topping zapped a dormant circuit in my brain. Immediately my body screamed for more. If one slice could feel that good, then two would be even better. Reluctantly she gave me another piece. I inhaled it, savoring the textures and the mood lift. Just one more chunk and my world would be perfect. Weaseling one last slice was difficult but successful. The high was too short.

During my years in elementary school, Saturday was the jubilee of each week. The closest store was a two mile round trip. With carefully saved change from my allowance I race-walked to my sugar supplier. Rain, snow or single-digit temperatures never impeded me. Arriving home from my expedition, I snuck down to the basement and gulped down all my treasure. I did not share. Junior High was even better. A small family grocery store was across the street from school. Every morning I paced the buckled sidewalk out front, waiting for it to open to get my fix. During classes I stuffed myself with gum, hard candy and jelly beans. My teachers busted me and complained to my folks. I suffered from heartburn and sleeplessness. I refused to cut down or stop.

An overnight high school band trip. Two hours to kill before dinner. My roommate had stolen some bourbon from his parents and offered me some mixed with 7-UP. Candy didn't give me that wonderful inner warmth. Three drinks later I was a calm, funny, confident guy, ready to take on the world.

After my seventeenth birthday I got a job playing drums in a traveling lounge act. The combination of stage fright and homesickness was debilitating. A couple of beers enabled me to perform. More after work put me to sleep. Unknowingly, I had just stepped onto the hamster wheel of addiction.

The next twelve years were a dizzying descent into darkness. I morphed into a whining, depressed, angry man. Minimum wage jobs were sandwiched between thousands of miles of road trips. Eight drinks and I wanted nine. I woke up sick and fearful every morning. My cadaver eyes and bloated face a Halloween mask. I kept on drinking, rationalizing that anyone who lived my life would be drunk everyday too.

The epiphany came in the N.C.O club at Fort Lewis. I was propped up on a bench in the lobby. Beer number sixteen was in my left hand and my fiftieth cigarette was in my right. Did I want to die, or did I just want the pain to stop?

Three hours later, I checked into a hospital.

Ice-Cold Jimmy

Tuberculosis. That's what the hospital was used for back in the late 1940's. Now it was a lockdown ward for alcoholics and drug addicts. Sick and tired of being sick and tired, I checked in for thirty days.

Foul odor of withdrawal sweat. Stale cigarette smoke. Eye-watering disinfectant. The rooms were painted tea-green. Steel mesh windows with a view of ventilation ducts and a corrugated tin roof. Just enough space for a twin bed and sink. The first day was detox. Nurses checked my blood pressure every hour. Handfuls of vitamins. Cold eggs, tepid decaf coffee, whole-wheat toast. All the soft drinks you wanted. Chest x-ray, liver function test, EKG. Isolation. Nerves howling, I settled in for the night. The fire alarm went off.

A nurse stuck his head in my room and yelled, "No problem man, I got you covered!" His name was James Doogan, aka "Ice Cold" Jimmy. Six-foot-seven, broken nose, prison ink. He looked like a hard luck Santa Claus.

"Mrs. Yamasaki set her wastebasket on fire 'cause I wouldn't give her any morphine," he said. Trembling, I crawled onto my cot. "You want some Librium?" Jimmy asked. "It'll smooth the kinks out."

"No thanks, I just need some sleep."

"Okay then, tomorrow you join the general population." He lumbered off down the corridor, boots echoing on the hard floor.

The general population: teenage heroin abusers. Sleek yuppie cocaine addicts wearing designer clothes, end stage alcoholics circling the drain. Breakfast at seven a.m., group therapy at nine, exercise period at eleven and lunch at noon. Between lunch and dinner were individual sessions with psychologists and lectures about the disease of addiction. Evenings we were driven to meetings at churches and community centers to prepare us for re-entry into society. Jimmy was everywhere. He ate with us, worked out with us, listened tirelessly, his empathy unlimited. He had served five years for manslaughter, sobered up and put himself through nursing school working nights as a janitor. We were lucky to have him around.

Eight a.m. on day thirty-one, I gave the staff my home and work numbers and left the hospital. Five-thirty that afternoon, I was setting up my drums in a cocktail lounge to begin a two week engagement. Ice cubes tinkled, the sweet aromas of wine and brandy, icy mugs of beer. Opening nights were always stressful. I walked to the bar. A waitress signaled that I had a phone call. "How ya doin' man?" boomed Ice Cold Jimmy. I told him that a relapse was imminent. "I know it's tough. The disease is cunning, baffling and powerful. Eat somethin' sweet and call me every hour." Lemon pie, black coffee and the phone calls kept me sober that evening. We never spoke again. Jimmy Doogan was murdered in a tavern parking lot two nights later.

Killer, ex-con … guardian angel.

Clean

A BRAND NEW LIFE. Sober. I was employed, had an apartment and a car. But a black fog rolled in with a vengeance, determined to strangle my recovery.

Anxiety. No energy. My sense of humor replaced by mean spirited cynicism. Violent mood swings, from seething anger to a fetal curl. Jim Beam had been banished and now I was alone battling the demons. At first I thought it was just my situation. Underemployed, living paycheck to paycheck. Six months later the pain was still there, and getting worse. No appetite. I shunned friends and family, beat myself up for not being strong enough to face the challenge.

Determined not to drink, I ran five miles a day and started lifting weights. Didn't feel any better. Went to Alcoholics Anonymous. No one would sponsor me. I completely shut down. Life is so much easier when you don't give a damn. Anger and self-pity festered under the numbness. Persistent dark fantasies. Exhausted and suicidal, it was one bad day after another.

I crashed and burned at work.

One bleak winter morning, my boss caught me sitting with my head in my hands, crying like a baby. She gave me a choice: get some help, or lose the job. Spurred by the threat of unemployment, I called my doctor and asked for a referral to a therapist.

He must have picked one out of the Yellow Pages.

The neighborhood was ominous. Mentally ill screaming at light poles, street-kid predators hanging out on the corners, stripped cars. The address was scrawled over a door between a porn shop and a bail bondsman. Broken glass scrunched under my tires as I parked. The meter had been mugged for change. After running a gauntlet of panhandlers, I was inside.

Metronome rhythm of dripping water. Sticky yellow linoleum. Light bulbs scowled through bug-crusted fixtures, pale blue paint flaked off the walls. Not a soul in sight. There were four doors in the hall. "Phil Krebs, P.H.D." was painted on the nearest one.

The office had a couple of spindly mismatched chairs and a coffee table tattooed with cigarette burns. Smells of burnt toast and mildew hung in the air. On the table was a form with my name typed at the top and a note to fill it out. Medical and family history, the reason for my visit. Twenty minutes later, Dr. Krebs sidled in through a back door and sat down next to me.

A gangly pot-bellied man, dressed in a sagging grey sweat suit. White Hippie hair and beard. Probably seventy years old. Brand new tennis shoes. Nauseating cologne. He glanced at the form and looked at me expectantly.

Staring at the floor, I let it out. How life was so unfair. How I had quit drinking and felt like crap. Every time I looked up he was admiring his shoes. He said nothing. I finished my tirade and asked him what I should do. In a bored monotone, he suggested that I quit my job and get another one. Then he handed me a bill for 120 dollars. I ripped up the invoice. Eyes blazing, I stomped out to my car. The street urchins gave me a wide berth.

I went back to A.A. Ninety meetings in ninety days. After twenty, I could enjoy food. Sixty days and I could laugh.

The ninetieth, I watched the moon rise.

Back to Square One

I WAS TRAVELING WITH A JAZZ TRIO and hoping for a record deal. I'd been clean ten years.

I was working in Aberdeen, Washington. Summer had turned the Evergreens toast-brown. You could smell the Pacific, hear the gulls. People complained about the shake mill shutting down. Unemployment was fifty percent. Everybody was into Marlboros, pick-up trucks, Jack Daniels, rifles. My gig was in the bar at the Denny's. Chips in the glasses, burns in the rug, spiders in the light fixtures. The odor of Lysol mixed with candle wax. My pay was fifty bucks a night plus coffee at the breaks and one free beef sandwich in the restaurant.

I was sitting at the bar after the third set on a dismal Tuesday night. Gripping a club soda and lime, staring at my reflection in the mirror behind the bottles. I looked seedy and pale. Things were TOO SHARP. "Gimme a shot of Beam, Ron!" I barked.

The first drink was sunshine. The second, orgasmic. I drank the third on stage.

Not caring about the crowd, I picked *Straight No Chaser* for the first tune. The piece was crazy fast with obtuse breaks.

I closed my eyes and dove into the music. The sticks felt light as balsa. The snare drum was crunchy, the tom-toms a primal roar, the cymbals rain and lightning. Fresh ideas flowed. The rest of the set was dynamite. We closed with the ballad *It Never Entered My Mind*. I teased and caressed the melody, brought out the passion and melancholy. My best performance of the tour. I bought a fifth to go and swaggered back to the motel.

I jerked awake. Hot light pierced my eyes. The breeze stank of salt and seaweed, waves licked my forehead. No shoes, sodden socks, sand on my lips and bird shit on my jacket. My right hand was swollen and painful. Guts roiling, I eased into a standing position and got my bearings. I saw a trail trampled through the sea grass and followed it. My left shoe was leaning against the curb. Using my shirt for a sling, I limped down the road. A green and white sign said, "Aberdeen One Mile."

Inside my room was a fist-sized hole in the wall. The empty fifth floated in the toilet. After cleaning up I choked down some beer and soup, went to the town's physician/veterinarian. The good news: no broken bones and a Vicodin prescription. The bad news: it would take six weeks to heal. Performing was out of the question. I called the other musicians and told them I couldn't finish the gig, paid the desk clerk twenty bucks to load the Chevy, chugged a quart of Coors and aimed for home.

A week-long bender decimated my savings. The rent was due. My hand felt better, but I couldn't play my instrument. I went to St. Vinnies and bought a white shirt and black slacks. Picked up an evening paper and cruised the want ads. The Mexican place down the block needed a dishwasher. In the morning I had a breakfast of bourbon and breath mints and walked over for an interview.

'Pepe's Hideaway' was stuffed between a dry cleaner and a tire store. The place was homey and clean inside. Real flowers, muted guitar track. The delicious smell of corn and tomatoes and roasted chicken. A narrow Japanese man in a navy suit was studying register tape. Black fly-away hair capped an acorn face. I cleared my throat. "You here about job?" he asked. I nodded. "I Arnold Noguchi, ownah. Fill out this form, bring to me." I complied. "You only people show up. You hired. Two rule: You late, you fired. You lazy, you fired. Okay?" he said.

"Yessir."

Working in the kitchen was like lifting weights in a sauna. The hangovers were crippling. With no booze on the job my brain was boiling at the end of the day. By now two drinks meant twelve. One night a small black dragon scurried out of the closet. Orange eyes, spiky hide, vapor from its nostrils. I grabbed a butcher knife and chased it around the apartment. It crawled under the bed, purred. I locked myself in the bathroom and slept in the tub. The new day brought what alcoholics refer to as a "moment of clarity." It was time to crawl out of the murk.

Cold turkey was hell. Anxiety and depression strangled me. Gallons of coffee and pounds of chocolate did nothing to curb the craving for alcohol. Forty-eight hours without a drink and I was climbing the walls. Thinking some air would help, I took a walk around the neighborhood and found myself in front of a church. The door was open, the sanctuary empty. Waning light cast rainbows through the stained glass. The air was cool and soothing. I realized that I couldn't recover by myself. I turned my life over to a Higher Power and took one day at a time.

It took five years for me to get one year of sobriety.

Manager

A ninety three unit condo complex in North Seattle. Cream and green and tired. I accepted the resident manager job because of the flexible hours and the rent-free apartment.

This morning there was urine in a stairwell, vomit in the lobby. Condoms and broken liquor bottles strewn in the parking lot. Women's underwear flapped on the fence.

I was sweeping up the glass when the owner of 203 walked over. Cue-ball complexion, orange and vermillion mu-mu hanging on a linebacker's frame. Elderly. She waved a pair of fluorescent tubes in my face. "The light in the elevator makes my skin look pale. Here are some new lamps. Please put these in NOW!" An hour later, she called and said the new lighting didn't help, please put back the original lighting and return her tubes.

While vacuuming a hallway, the owner of 115 interrupted me. A tiny man who's a long haul trucker. Stained T-shirt, cowboy boots, filthy jeans. His fingernails were fierce-blue, mauve eye shadow flaked over false lashes. Whiskey fumes tweaked my nose. He complained about a dry rhododendron in his backyard. I set up a sprinkler. My cell rang. The night shift nurse in 311. She said she couldn't sleep with the sprinkler running. I explained about the dry rhodie. She said, "Thanks for nothing." Hung up on me.

An appliance delivery for the secretary in 221 was three hours overdue. A call from the front door. Broken English, dial tone. I ran out and saw a box truck. Two scary guys with neck tattoos and clipboards were pounding on the intercom. I let them in, gave directions, then left to degrease a parking stall. When I returned, they had scratched all the fire doors, put a five inch gouge in a wall, and smashed a light fixture.

Next was handling a barking dog complaint, politely asking the Vietnam vet from 330 not to smoke pot in the exercise room and digging chocolate cake out of the carpet. Cell rang. 107 asked me if I knew about the commotion in the back lot.

A female voice yelled obscenities. A male voice whimpered. The brother and sister who lived in 202 were wrestling on the asphalt. Scratching, biting and spitting like alley cats. While I was calling 911, the carpenter from 104 rolled in. Big lumpy moron with a hellfire temper. He screeched to a halt and yelled, "Leave her alone buddy!" Claw hammer in hand, he jumped between them. The brother twisted the tool from the guy's grip. Sister began kicking him in the groin. They all went to jail.

After supper I went up on the roof and tried to decompress. A sizzling summer evening. Grease smoke from the neighborhood restaurants tangled with car exhaust. Non-stop sirens, dog arias. I wanted to quit. I lit a cigarette and watched the setting sun shave away daylight.

There was a white rose taped to my apartment door. And an envelope. Inside, a fifty dollar bill with a note: "Thank you so much for everything you do around here. We are so lucky to have you." It was signed, "The light tube lady."

Postscripts

Exterminator

Three fifteen a.m. SLAM … SLAMSLAM! Dave Stone's neighbor had arrived, banging all the doors on his van. He was always drunk, laughing and singing at the top of his lungs. Woke up the whole neighborhood seven days a week. Dave thought about a line from the Serenity Prayer: "The courage to change the things I can." Three o'clock the next morning, he was waiting in the parking lot.

Moonlight blared, the air was thin and warm. The van pulled in and parked. A dark skinny guy stumbled out jingling keys. Hog-eyed with a stupid mouth. Probably forty. Greasy pants, no shirt, shit-kicker boots. He saw Dave and nodded and jammed a key into the door lock. Dave broke his nose with the palm of his hand. It sounded like stepping on a bag of pretzels. Stunned and bloody, the guy collapsed onto the blacktop. Dave snapped his neck with a vicious twist. Looked around for witnesses. No lights behind the windows of the buildings, nobody in sight. Dave yanked the keys out of the door, opened the back of the van and threw the guy in. He jumped into the driver's seat and drove to the airport and left the van in the parking garage. Whistling, *New York, New York,* he sauntered to the cab stand for a ride home.

The apartment he lived in was provided by his company. Old solid furniture, glassy wood flooring, fresh white walls. New kitchen appliances and a garden view. He put the kettle on.

For Dave, killing people was simply doing God's work. He wasn't a drooling psychopath fulfilling fantasies born from an abusive childhood. Planning murder never occurred to him. His victims were provided by the Man Upstairs. The kettle screamed and Dave brewed Earl Grey.

After a dull day at work he changed into jeans, a frayed blue sweatshirt and black jogging shoes and drove over to the neighborhood lounge in his grumbling V.W. The late summer light was fading, he could smell fall approaching. He sat on a stool at the bar and ordered a draft and French fries. The bartender barely glanced at him. Dave was the definition of unremarkable. Tall, thin and white with a silver buzz cut and good teeth. Age had sketched lines on his face but he looked ten years younger than his fifty-five years. The combination of the hot salty potatoes and cold beer made him smile. The simple pleasures of life, he thought. He had one more draft, fired up the bug and cruised home through back streets.

Dave was driving slowly through an alley when he saw the bum. He was sitting on the ground propped up against a chain-link fence. Fat and dirty and snoring, an empty bottle in his fist. Cat-quiet, Dave got out of his car. The guy stank. He crushed the wino's neck and shoved the body behind a hedge. He crossed himself and gave thanks for the opportunity to help.

That night, in the gray area between rest and sleep, he reflected on his life. He felt lucky to have been raised in an Irish working class family, was grateful that he didn't have siblings. Dada had instilled in him the necessity of discipline and higher education. He went to school, studied hard. His career allowed him to travel and meet new people. He enjoyed free rent, free food and transportation. I am truly blessed, he thought.

The next day Dave was in a restaurant having lunch. Tuna on rye, split-pea soup, pecan pie. A commotion at the cash register. Claiming his bill wasn't right, a customer called the checker a "stupid whore," and threw money at her. Dave paid for his meal, said something to comfort the waitress and followed him out the door. The customer was dressed in a beautifully tailored brown suit. Huge gold wristwatch, rings glinted on both hands. He walked to a brand new Cadillac parked out of sight behind the café. Usually Dave didn't use a weapon, but he always carried an ice pick in case his target was bigger and stronger than he was. When Brown Suit bent to open the car door, Dave rammed the pick into the guy's right ear. He slid the body under the car.

The following Sunday Dave Stone dressed in his work clothes for his last shift in town. He'd been here for six months, the usual time. He was being transferred to another district Monday. He decided to walk and chose a wool cap and light gloves. Dry leaves danced on the wet sidewalk. Clouds of birds floated south. With a spring in his step, Dave entered the building and sat in the booth. Took a deep breath and cracked his knuckles. A high nervous voice sifted through the grille in front of him.

"Forgive me Father, I have sinned."

Classy and Sick

His radio was on. Wagner soaked the room. Chauncey was tall and shaped like a mallet. Meat-fat white with kiss-me lips. Short blonde hair, gray eyes flecked with mirth. He pulled the cake from the oven and inhaled the luscious chocolate fragrance. Bobbing his head along with the brass, he thinned the marzipan frosting with slug bait. Decided to dress while the cake cooled. Magenta push-up bra and thong. The stockings were sheer and black. A charcoal dress and long, red wig. Ruby studs in his ears. He'd applied the make-up first thing in the morning, used a model in a magazine for a guide. He slipped into deep blue stiletto heels, iced and packed the confection in a plastic case, shrugged into a fox jacket. He placed the case on the passenger seat of the stolen Jaguar, cranked the engine and drove to the fund-raiser.

The Convention Center had just been remodeled into a luxurious red-gold cavern. In the foyer local politicians, corporate magnates and young social climbers glad-handed, drank champagne and talked too loud. He set the cake on the buffet. Accepted the thanks of some dried out matrons who reeked of Chanel. He wiggled back to the car and drove to the rent by-the-week apartment. Parked in the fire lane, left the car unlocked with the keys in the ignition. He went inside, removed the make-up and changed into loose jeans, running shoes and his favorite hooded sweatshirt. Stashed the disguise in a duffel bag, tucked his toothbrush in a pants pocket and rode a bus to the warehouse to pick up his next load.

Kitty litter going to San Francisco. He smoked and bounced in the plush cab of the tractor-trailer. Reveled in the freedom of the open road. Cresting the Grapevine, sunrise was the color of forest fire. Fifty miles south of Eureka, he pulled into a truck stop. The breakfast rush was over, so he was alone at the counter. An elderly couple argued in a back booth. A beat up T.V. hung over the pick-up window: ESPN with the sound off. Rattling dishes and sizzling from the kitchen. The stressed-out waitress took his order for brains and eggs, French toast with grape jelly, coffee regular. He glanced at a newspaper left on the stool next to him.

"V.I.P.'S POISONED AT BENEFIT! TWO DEAD!" the headline announced. Chauncey smirked. V.I.P.'s. indeed, he thought. The rich never accepted the insignificance of their lives. Flora, the food server, set down his order, saw what he was reading. Said, "There sure are some crazies out there huh?"

Shaking his head, Chauncey replied, "Yes ma'm. May I have more coffee? And some ketchup please."

"Right away darlin', anythin' else?"

"Just a smile ma'm." She hesitated, confused. Then cracked a grin.

"Thank-you, you're so pretty when you smile," he said. He ate the meal, paid the bill and tipped big. Motored down the interstate.

After unloading, he picked up some ice blocks to drive across town to a country club. The California sun was high and blazing, the Marine Layer a memory. Stop and go traffic all the way to the gates. The gateman checked the delivery on his clipboard and waved him through. Steep straight lane into paradise. Shamrock-green lawn to infinity. Flower beds packed with pastel colors. The chick-chick-chick of the sprinklers the only sound in the thick rich quiet. The clubhouse was modern looking with Spanish-tiled steeples and circular windows. Chauncey idled around to the service entrance. Backed into a bay. Watched a crew of apron-clad Mexicans hump the ice into the kitchen. He wandered out front. Brand new gold BMW sedan straddled two parking slots. He used the leather punch on his pocket knife to perforate the brake lines. He bought the Mexicans a few beers, cruised back through the gate and parked on the shoulder. Between his second and third cigarettes, the Beemer screamed down the driveway and smashed through the gate. Must have been traveling over seventy miles an hour. The driver missed the corner and rolled it over a guard rail. Roaring fireball. Chauncey made a Y-turn and drove back towards town and checked into a Holiday Inn.

He was in the mood for an expensive dinner. Looked through the Yellow Pages, found a steak house that touted, "Panoramic Views and Gourmet Dining," and made a reservation. He shaved carefully, put on a snappy pinstriped Italian suit, buffed his loafers to a diamond sparkle and called a taxi.

The hyper maître d´ ushered him into the bar. He spoke with a foreign accent. "It will be a few minutes until your table is ready, sir. Have a cocktail and I will come for you when it is ready." The lounge was still. Masculine furnishings. Just a couple of other patrons waiting for space in the dining room. Chauncey ordered a vodka martini up with a twist, munched some cashews. The city twinkled through the glass walls. He struck up a conversation with a pretty brunette sitting two spaces down. Her name was Aida. She was curvy, pale and warm. Captivating violet irises under luxurious lashes. Her hip-slit gown matched her eyes, her laughter was music. Perfect, he thought.

They shared a table, discussed politics and the stock market, Renoir and Picasso. Enjoyed each other's company. The food was first rate, the wine bold. Chauncey paid the check and offered to walk her to her car. She accepted.

The lot was deserted. Aida drove a cute British sports car. Chauncey took her keys and opened the driver's door. She looked deeply into his eyes and said, "I knew I could trust you the moment I met you."

Author

CRIMSON MOUNTAINS. Demons munching children. Sulfur and screams in the air. A rattling rumble yanked him from the nightmare. The 5:15 a.m. bus had arrived at the stop under his bedroom window. Percy Konitz untangled himself from the wet sheets and staggered into the bathroom. Cockroaches fled the light. Ancient green linoleum popped under his bare feet, sewer gas from the toilet. Hot water ran out after four minutes. No matter, he thought, today is my last day. He put on yesterday's clothes, locked up the apartment, threw the keys in the recycle bin.

He walked to work. The morning air was warm and sweet, the sun a white diamond. Rush hour traffic crept along the downtown streets. Hostile horns, blown mufflers. His twenty-fifth birthday.

His formative years were spent as the only child of a working class couple. Dad was a tool and die worker, Mom a housewife and part time cosmetologist. They lived in a close knit neighborhood, went to church every Sunday.

One stormy autumn evening when he was nine, the family was in the living room watching the news. Hot chocolate, sugar cookies, rain sluicing down the windows. A man had been murdered. The newscaster said, "Clarence Ramsey was attacked behind the building he cleaned and suffered multiple stab wounds. The police are investigating and doing a nation-wide search for the perpetrator. If anyone has any information, call 911." Shocked, Percy asked his Dad how somebody could do such a thing. "There's evil in this world son, always will be. The important thing to remember is that evil flourishes when good people do nothing." Percy wrote that down and taped it to his mirror.

At thirteen, Percy was big and kind and bright, an honor student. His quick mind and sense of humor endeared him to his classmates and teachers. When asked about his future, he would respond: "I want to study writing, or maybe the mind." Percy loved life.

New neighbors next door. A single mother and son. Jason was Percy's age. That was the only similarity. Jason was loud and nasty and arrogant. Houses were burglarized. Obscenities were spray painted on light poles and garages. Flowers and shrubs were torn up, cars vandalized. Excrement on people's porches. When Jason's mother was questioned, she said, "You bastards have no proof it's my Jason. He a good boy. Leave us the hell alone!" The whole community was wound tight.

On a Friday afternoon, Percy walked home from school, taking the long route through the ball field. Lazy sunlight, the late spring fragrance of hot dust and flowers. He heard a sound like a ball hitting a back stop. He peered around a cor-ner and saw Jason throwing a kitten against a wall. The animal had obviously died, but he kept pulverizing it, whooping and sniggering. He didn't see Percy.

Later that evening, Percy hid in the alley next to Jason's house. He knew Jason drank beer and smoked cigarettes there before going to bed. When Jason was rummy, Percy sneaked up behind him and choked him unconscious. With the kitten's image in his mind, he slammed Jason's head repeatedly against the concrete and crushed his skull. Calmly went inside and called the police. He was arrested, booked and put in a holding cell. Pled guilty to aggravated assault. Because of his age and lack of remorse, the judge sentenced Percy to a psychiatric ward until he turned twenty four. If at that time he was still deemed a threat to himself or others, he could be locked up indefinitely. His parents wept as he was led from the courtroom.

Percy bloomed during his incarceration. He was taking college level courses at fifteen. Read Camus and listened to opera. Earned a masters degree in Creative Writing and a bachelors in Psychology. The staff loved the quiet boy. His folks visited every week. On a winter night, their car spun on some black ice and went over an embankment. Both perished. Doctors and nurses rallied around him and became surrogate parents. Percy was doing so well the judge released him. Due to his felony conviction, the only job he could get was sorting and filing in the records department of an insurance company. Everyone avoided him. He disconnected.

Percy climbed the stairs for the final time to the office break room. He was always the first one in, so he was responsible for making coffee. He set up the machine. Through the window he watched hummingbirds play, the landscape crew busy on the grounds. Percy's supervisor bulled through the door.

Frank Cadera was forty-three years old. Bleached teeth, square head, rampant nose hair. Short guy who bragged about his suits and played grab-ass with the female employees.

"Mornin' convict," he said. "Coffee ready yet?"

"Yes sir, regular or decaf?" Percy replied.

"Reg'lar, and hurry up, I don't have all damn day!" Percy poured the pot of scalding coffee over Frank's head and kicked him twice in the balls.

Percy Konitz received a sentence of twenty years to life at Eastern State Hospital. His autobiography *Rhythms of Violence* became a *New York Times* bestseller.

About the author

Eugene Babb was a professional musician for thirty years. He has a B.A. in Sociology and is currently managing a condominium complex in Seattle, Washington.

9 781609 441012